Unlikely
SANTA

AN AMISH CHRISTMAS STORY

JENNIFER
SPREDEMANN

Published in Indiana by *Blessed Publishing*.
www.jebspredemann.com

All Scripture quotations are taken from the King James Version of the Holy Bible.

Cover design by *iCreate Designs* ©
Formatting by Polgarus Studio

ISBN: 978-1-940492-50-6
10 9 8 7 6 5 4 3 2 1

BOOKS by JENNIFER SPREDEMANN

Learning to Love – Saul's Story
(Sequel to Chloe's Revelation)

AMISH BY ACCIDENT TRILOGY

Amish by Accident
*Englisch on Purpose (*Prequel to *Amish by Accident)*
*Christmas in Paradise (*Sequel to *Amish by Accident*)
(co-authored with Brandi Gabriel)

AMISH SECRETS SERIES

An Unforgivable Secret - Amish Secrets 1
A Secret Encounter - Amish Secrets 2
A Secret of the Heart - Amish Secrets 3
An Undeniable Secret - Amish Secrets 4
A Secret Sacrifice - Amish Secrets 5
(co-authored with Brandi Gabriel)
A Secret of the Soul - Amish Secrets 6
A Secret Christmas – Amish Secrets 2.5
(co-authored with Brandi Gabriel)

AMISH BIBLE ROMANCES

An Amish Reward
An Amish Deception
An Amish Honor
An Amish Blessing
An Amish Betrayal

NOVELETTES

Cindy's Story – An Amish Fairly Tale Novelette 1
Rosabelle's Story – An Amish Fairly Tale Novelette 2

OTHER

Love Impossible
Unlikely Santa

COMING 2020 (Lord Willing)

The Trespasser (Amish Country Brides)
The Heartbreaker (Amish Country Brides)
The Charmer (Amish Country Brides)
The Drifter (Amish Country Brides)

BOOKS by J.E.B. SPREDEMANN

Unofficial Glossary
of Pennsylvania Dutch Words

Ach – Oh

Aldi – Girlfriend

Bann – Shunning

Boppli/Bopplin – Baby/Babies

Bu – Boy

Daed/Dat – Dad

Grossdawdi – Grandfather

Denki – Thanks

Der Herr – The Lord

Dummkopp – Dummy

Englisch(er) – A non-Amish person

Fraa – Wife

G'may – Members of an Amish fellowship

Gott – God

Gross sohn – Grandson

Gut – Good

Jah – Yes

Kapp – Amish head covering

Kinner – Children

Kinskind – Grandchild

Maedel – Girl

Mamm – Mom

Nee – No

Schatzi – Sweetheart

Wunderbaar – Wonderful

Author's Note

It should be noted that the Amish people and their communities differ one from another. There are, in fact, no two Amish communities exactly alike. It is this premise on which this book is written. We have taken cautious steps to assure the authenticity of Amish practices and customs. Both Old Order Amish and New Order Amish are portrayed in this work of fiction and may be inconsistent with some Amish communities.

We, as *Englischers*, can learn a lot from the Plain People and their simple way of life. Their hard work, close-knit family life, and concern for others are to be applauded. As the Lord wills, may this special culture continue to be respected and remain so for many centuries to come.

If you're interested in learning more about the differences in Amish culture, please refer to my blog post *That's Not Amish!*

To my Lord and Saviour, Jesus Christ,
May the words of my mouth, the meditation of my
heart, and works of my hands bring You glory.

PROLOGUE

Shannon Parker beamed as she strolled into the kitchen this beautiful Sunday morning. Life was finally beginning! She'd graduated high school a couple of months ago. She had a decent waitressing job that provided enough money for her to set some aside for the future—a future that seemed very promising at the moment.

Especially since Aiden had said he'd been thinking about taking their relationship to the next level. Her heart flipped at the thought of what he meant by that. Was he thinking of proposing? They'd been dating for a year, so it *was* possible.

Mom and Dad had gone out of town to celebrate their twentieth wedding anniversary, which left her the one in charge of her three younger siblings. She'd always thought she had a fantastic family. They weren't well-off and they didn't live in the fanciest house in town, but they all got along and respected each other. It wasn't a perfect family, by any means, but pretty good considering the stories she'd heard about some of her friends from school. She was satisfied with her life. Thankful, even.

Her cell phone buzzed and she pulled it from her pocket. She expected it to be Aiden. Instead it was an unread text from Mom. *Had a great time! On our way home now. See you soon. Love you!*

She quickly texted back. *K. Love you too!*

She hummed as she pulled the eggs out of the fridge and began preparing breakfast for her charges. She'd wake them up in a little bit. Right now, she'd enjoy the quiet time alone.

Several hours later, a knock on the door told her Aiden might be making a surprise visit. He did that once in a while. She'd always loved his surprises.

She pulled the front door open.

"Are you Shannon Parker?" It wasn't Aiden.

She stared wide-eyed at the uniformed officer and his partner. They wanted to see *her*? She hadn't done anything to warrant a visit from the police. Had she? She combed her mind.

"Miss?" He repeated.

She shook her head, just realizing she hadn't answered the man. "Um, yeah. That's me. May I...help you?" Her hands slightly trembled. They always seemed to do that whenever a law enforcement officer was near. Not that she'd had all that much experience with the police. But the one time she'd been pulled over because her taillight was out, she'd had the same reaction.

"Your parents are Marie and Andrew Parker, correct?" he asked.

"Yes..." Her brow lowered. Why all these questions?

"Miss Parker, we have some bad news, I'm afraid." The officer fidgeted a moment and briefly glanced at the other officer before training his eyes back on her. "Your parents were in a head-on collision early this afternoon. I'm really sorry to tell you this, but neither of them survived. They both died at the scene of the accident..." The officer had continued speaking, but Shannon hadn't heard another word.

Mom and Dad were...*dead*? She shook her head. No, that couldn't be right. It wasn't. She was just dreaming. It had to be some sort of nightmare. Surely she'd awaken at any moment.

A warm but calloused hand rested on her forearm and she looked up. Into the eyes of an officer. It wasn't a dream. *It's not a dream. God? No. Please.*

"Are you all right, miss?"

All right? She wanted to scream at this man, "No, I'm *not* all right! You just told me my parents are dead! I'll never be all right again!" But she didn't scream. Instead, she remained silent, keeping her words bottled up inside.

Moisture gathered in her eyes and inevitably spilled over onto her cheeks as reality finally set in. She quickly glanced back to see if any of the other children were present. They must've all been cleaning their rooms like she'd suggested in preparation for Mom and Dad's arrival. But now that wouldn't happen. Mom and Dad would never again drive up to their home. They'd never again walk through the front door. They'd never again gather her and her siblings in their arms and tell them they loved them.

Dad wouldn't be there to walk her down the aisle.

Mom wouldn't be present to help her find the perfect wedding gown. To give her advice for marriage and raising her own babies.

What on earth was she going to do now? She couldn't do this alone.

An officer led her to the couch, where she collapsed in tears. She no longer possessed the strength to stand. Her two younger siblings rushed out of their rooms when they heard the commotion. Little Melanie would be too young to understand, but Brighton and Jaycee surely would. She repeated the officer's words, then opened her arms to her brothers. The threesome bawled, and sobbed, and comforted each other until well into the evening. And the next day. And the next. Each day, they slowly came to grips with their grave reality.

Mom and Dad were never coming back.

ONE

Late November, the same year…

"Judy, I got the buggy all hitched up! You ready to go yet?" Bishop Christopher Stoltz called from the back door of their home.

"In a minute, *schatzi*. I *chust* need to double check my list." Her melodic voice wafted from the kitchen window.

"Ah…so you're making a list and checking it twice." He chuckled, stroking his white beard. Jolliness bubbled up in his soul this morning, for some reason. Perhaps it was the fact that they just had Thanksgiving and Christmas was approaching. That always put him in a chipper mood.

Judy finally appeared and met him at the carriage. "I think I'm ready now."

"Have you figured out who's been naughty or nice?"

He assisted his wife as she stepped up into the buggy, then rounded Prancer and hopped in himself.

"What foolishness are you speaking, husband?" She frowned.

"*Ach*, nothing." He set the buggy in motion with a slight flick of his wrist, gently holding the reins, amusement sparkling in his eyes.

Shannon Parker pushed the shopping cart down the Walmart aisle, making sure her three siblings were still within sight. The youngest, twenty-two-month-old Melanie, sat fastened in the cart's seat while the other two walked alongside and sometimes ahead of the cart.

She dug into her purse and counted her money once again. She grimaced. There was no way she'd be able to purchase all the items she'd planned for. She'd just have to figure out a way to stretch their meals—again.

She picked up a bag of dry beans—they'd last for at least two meals, and some rice. Rice was great for stretching the budget and filling bellies, she'd learned. It could also be used for breakfast, lunch, or dinner. She grabbed another bag.

"Do we have to eat beans and rice again?" Five-year-old Jaycee complained, like he often did.

"Just be thankful we have food to eat. My cooking isn't that bad, is it?" Her brow shot up.

"Well, it sure ain't as good as Mom's was."

"*Isn't* as good as Mom's was." She planted a hand on her hip. "Well, I'm sure that by the time I'm the age Mom was, I'll be a better cook. But for now, too bad. You'll just have to suffer through it."

"Can I get a candy bar?" He whined.

"*May* I get a candy bar? And no, you may not. We're on a limited budget. Besides, all that sugar isn't good for you."

"You sound like Mom."

"Good. Maybe you'll start listening to me then."

He reached for a candy bar and slyly placed it into the cart.

"I said no. We don't have the money right now, Jaycee." She removed the candy bar and put in back on the shelf.

"We never have the money." Tears filled his eyes.

She crouched down next to him and brushed away his tears. "I know it's hard right now, but we'll get through this, okay? I'm going to ask my boss if he'll give me a raise next week."

"And then we'll have money for a candy bar?"

"Maybe once in a while." She handed him a tissue. "Here, wipe your nose."

He did as told, then handed the tissue back to Shannon.

"Keep it in your pocket in case you need it again."

"Do you think Santa will get me a candy bar?" He perked up a little.

"Honey, Santa…" No, she wouldn't tell him the truth about Santa Claus. At least, not yet. They'd still been reeling from the death of their parents three months ago. She wasn't sure if Jaycee would be able to handle hearing the truth at this moment in time. He'd likely be devastated. "You can ask Santa when we go see him, okay?"

"We're going to see Santa Claus?" His mouth stood agape and his eyes sparkled with pure excitement. It was the happiest face she'd seen on her youngest brother since their parents died. They needed more happy times.

"That's right."

"When? When? Today?" He jumped up and down.

"I don't think Santa's in his house yet. We'll have to wait until December."

"When is that?"

"Next week." She frowned. She hadn't even contemplated what it would cost to get her siblings a gift for Christmas this year. It would be their most meager holiday celebration ever.

They'd gone out for a special meal on Thanksgiving

Day at the local restaurant where she'd worked most of her senior year. Her boss had provided a free meal for them, knowing her circumstances. That had been something to be thankful for.

She'd thought about preparing a fancy meal like Mom always had, but there was no way she wanted to put the effort in to create a gigantic meal with all the fixings. She could bake chicken, open a can of corn, and prepare macaroni and cheese out of the box, but she was not a skilled cook by any stretch of the word. She fixed meals so they could fill their bellies. At least they'd celebrated Thanksgiving, though. She'd managed to keep her tears at bay while the younger children were present, but she couldn't help remembering Thanksgivings of previous years. She never thought she'd have to do it on her own. Oh, how she'd taken Mom and Dad for granted!

"Are we almost done?" Jaycee moaned, shaking her out of her melancholy mood.

"Yes." She glanced around. "Where's your brother?" The eleven-year-old was nowhere in sight.

"I don't know. He said something about looking at fish. I want to look at fish too."

"Brighton," Shannon called. She maneuvered the cart around the corner but her brother wasn't there. Great, she'd lost Brighton! "Okay, we'll go see the fish, but let's look down every aisle so we can try to find your brother."

As they headed in that direction, Shannon made sure Jaycee stayed close to the cart so she didn't lose him too.

"There he is!" Jaycee proclaimed as they turned into the pet aisle. He raced toward his brother. "Shan was worried about you."

"Brighton, you know better than to go off by yourself like that. Don't you know there are bad people who are out there just waiting for children to wander off so they can snatch them away?"

He rolled his eyes. "You sound like Mom."

"I'm serious, Brighton. Next time, stay with me." She looked at him pointedly, communicating to him that she meant business.

"My fish need food." He reached for a can of flakes.

Shannon frowned at the price. "We can't buy that right now."

"But my fish will die. They ran out yesterday."

Shannon studied the cart and tried to determine which items to put back. "Only the small can."

"But the bigger one is a better deal."

"We don't have money for it." She shook her head. "Come on. Let's go now."

They headed to the register, but she'd lost count of the total. Oh well, if it was too much, she'd just ask the cashier to subtract something. She hated doing that, but it certainly wouldn't be the first time.

"Here we go." She picked a lane with only two customers ahead of her, the shortest one she could find.

"My feet hurt," Jaycee whined.

Shannon glanced beyond the register and spotted a bench. "Why don't you go sit there until we're through the line. And don't talk to strangers or go off with anyone."

"I won't."

She turned to Brighton. "Why don't you go with him?"

"Can I play a video game?" He pointed to the tiny arcade just beyond the bench where Jaycee went to sit.

"It's *may* I. And no, I don't have extra money. As it is, we'll probably have to put stuff back."

"That's embarrassing, Shan."

"I know, but it is what it is."

Brighton dug into his pants pocket. "I think I might have a couple of quarters in my pocket. I'll give them to you if you think it will help."

She shook her head, her heart filling with gratefulness. "Thanks, but two quarters wouldn't do much. Go ahead and play your game."

She carefully eyed Jaycee until he was safely seated on the bench. An older Amish man shared the bench with him. Yeah, he would be safe.

13

TWO

Christopher sat patiently as Judy completed her shopping. He smiled as a young *Englisch* boy came and sat next to him.

"Hi! My name is Jaycee." The boy beamed up at him.

Christopher nodded in silence.

"Do you remember me?" Jaycee climbed up onto his lap as though he were his *kinskind*. "My sister said I would have to wait to see you until December. I guess she didn't know you'd be here today."

Christopher stroked his beard and cocked a brow.

The boy reached up and felt his beard, as though trying to decide whether it was real or not. He then poked at his glasses.

He chortled. "Have a care now. Don't want to smudge them up."

Jaycee nodded, his expression serious. "My momma

used to wear glasses too, just like me and you. But she don't need 'em no more 'cuz her and Daddy died in a car *askident*."

Compassion tugged at Christopher's heart and he frowned. "Your folks are…gone?"

Jaycee nodded. "Yep, I miss 'em real bad. I cried lots. We all did. Now Shannon has to watch us. She acts like Mom now. But sometimes she still cries." He pointed to a young woman who couldn't be more than a teenager.

"How old is Shannon?"

"My sister? She's eighteen, I think. My baby sister is gonna be two on her birthday. And my big brother is eleven. I'm five." His eyes grew large. "How old are *you*?"

"*Ach*, that doesn't matter." He chuckled.

"I'm supposed to tell you what I want for Christmas. Since my momma and daddy aren't here no more, I don't think Shan is going to get us anything. She'd don't have lots of money like Momma and Daddy had."

"What do you usually get for Christmas?"

Jaycee giggled. "Silly, you already know. You got it for me."

"I did?"

"Yep. Remember the Thomas train set?"

He shook his head.

16

"You have to remember. We live a little just past the post office. The house after you come over the hill. The white one." He shook his head in exasperation. "I didn't know Santa had a bad memory."

Christopher chuckled. "What were you hoping for this year?"

"Well, I'd really like for Momma and Daddy to come back home. But Shan says only God can do that, and she already *aksed* God and He said no." He stared at Christopher. "Why do you think God said no?"

Christopher shrugged. "It seems we only get one chance to live on this earth here. After we're gone, there's no coming back."

"But you know God, don't you? Maybe you can ask Him for me. He might listen to you better since you do a lot of nice things for people."

"I know God, but He will listen to you as much as to me."

"He will? But I can't see Him."

"I can't see Him either. I just pray."

"I prayed before." He glanced up as his sister was paying for the items in her cart. "I better go now. Could you maybe just get something special for my sister, or maybe give her a better job so she can buy me a candy bar next time?"

Christopher reached into his pocket and pulled out

his wallet. "You may get your candy bar now."

His eyes nearly jumped out of his glasses. "Really? Thank you, Santa!"

Jaycee leapt off the bench and hurried toward his sister. He turned back and waved with his entire arm.

Christopher chuckled and waved, then went in search of his *fraa*. Wouldn't Judy love to hear this tale?

Shannon handed the money over to the cashier, sighing in relief that she'd had enough. Barely.

Jaycee bounded toward her. "Here's money for my candy bar!" He thrust a dollar bill in her hand.

"Where'd you get that, Jaycee?"

"Santa gave it to me!" He nodded, then looked over at the bench he'd been sitting on. "Hey, where'd he go?"

"Maybe Rudolph swung by and picked him up," the impatient man in line behind them mumbled.

Shannon ignored him. He'd been making curt remarks since he'd gotten in line.

"Quickly, get your candy bar. We're holding up the line," she warned.

Jaycee dug into his pocket and pulled out what

looked to be a partially melted Snickers bar.

"Jaycee! You're not supposed to have that in your pocket."

The man in line behind them huffed.

She handed it to the cashier with an apologetic smile.

The cashier rang it up and handed the candy bar to Jaycee with amusement playing on her lips, along with the change.

"Thank you." Shannon pushed the cart past the register and headed toward the tiny arcade. "Go get your brother. Tell him we're leaving now."

"Okay," Jaycee mumbled around his half-eaten candy bar.

THREE

"**. . .** *a*nd that's what happened while I was waiting for you." Christopher finished sharing his shopping experience with his *fraa*. "Well, what do you think?"

A distressed look crossed Judy's face. "We need to do something to help them."

"I know, but what?" He scratched his chin. He'd been pondering the young family's predicament since he'd learned of it.

"Where do the young *kinner* go when the older one works?"

"School, I suppose."

"But you said there was a *boppli*, ain't so?"

"A two-year-old, I believe."

"I can't imagine she can work much with such responsibilities." Judy shook her head.

"*Jah*, they seemed to be struggling. Didn't buy

much food, by the look of it."

"Well, I suppose we could take him during the day."

"Her. It's a *maedel*. I'm not sure where the little one goes when the oldest one works."

"Do you know if they have relatives nearby? Maybe they watch the *boppli*."

"I wouldn't know. All I know is what the *bu* told me. Jaycee was his name." He chuckled. "And I think he believed I was Santa Claus."

Judy gasped. "Really?"

He nodded.

"What if we hired her at our roadside stand? Then she wouldn't have to worry about taking the *kinner* somewhere. I'm sure she would feel better knowing they are well cared for."

Christopher chuckled.

"What?"

He shrugged. "Well, they don't really know us. Not too sure she'd know they were well cared for."

"We can fix that. Where did you say they lived?"

"The *bu* said their house was past the post office. He didn't say which one, though."

"We'll just have to find out."

"Are you suggesting we go knock on doors?"

"Seems to me we could figure it out pretty easily by asking around." Judy tugged on her *kapp* string. "Now that I think about it, didn't someone mention an accident where the folks died some months back?"

"I suppose so."

Judy nodded. "We will find out where they live, then we will take them some treats. I'm sure the *kinner* will appreciate some of my special cookies."

Christopher nodded. His smile widened. "*I* appreciate your special cookies."

"And I could take over a couple of loaves of bread, some butter from Elsie, and some of my jam. Maybe pickles too. Do you think they'll like my pickles?"

"*I* like your pickles."

"Do you suppose they could use some quilts?"

"Now, Judy, let's not overdo it. We don't want to scare them away."

"I don't know anyone who'd be scared away by a quilt, husband."

"Maybe we'll *chust* bring some food at first. We can take a gander at their place while we're there and see if they need other things too."

"That sounds like a sensible idea."

"That's me. Always sensible."

"Let's not stretch the truth now, husband."

Christopher's eyes grew. "Me?"

"Always sensible? What about that time you brought that raccoon into the house?"

"He was hurt."

"He tore up the kitchen and ate all my fresh-made pies!"

Christopher chuckled. "He needed to eat too. Can't fault him for liking your pies. *I* like your pies."

"Easy for you to say when you didn't put all the work into making them. *Ach*, what am I going to do with you?"

"A *buss* would be nice." His eyes twinkled.

She leaned over and kiss him on the cheek.

FOUR

Shannon's cell phone buzzed in her back pocket. She quickly delivered the two plates of hot food to table number seven, then rushed back to check her messages. She'd left little Melanie with the teen neighbor girl and her poor baby sister had been screaming when she walked out the door this morning. She hated to leave her with someone she'd never stayed with, but she had no choice since the regular sitter called in sick.

She looked down at the phone in her hand. The message wasn't the babysitter. She didn't know if that was good or bad.

"Number seven asked for ketchup and a side of mayo," her coworker Shelby said.

"Okay, thanks." Shannon slipped the phone back into her pocket and rushed to get the condiments. She couldn't afford to lose out on a tip. Literally.

Brighton had just informed her that he needed new athletic shoes for school. He'd outgrown the sneakers he wore last year. Who knew how much those would cost. On top of using her gas, and traveling all the way to Walmart.

She sighed. Could anything else go wrong today?

"Customers at table number three," Shelby hollered over her shoulder while she whisked through the double doors to the kitchen.

Shannon glanced toward the table and tucked two menus under her arm. She walked to the table and sucked in a breath.

Oh, no. Not today. Her heart sped up.

"Hey, Shan. How's it going?" Aiden's smile was bright. As though he hadn't ripped her heart out two and a half months ago.

She attempted a friendly smile, but it felt wobbly. She would *not* cry.

"May I get you something to drink?" She instead focused on the young woman opposite her ex. His new girlfriend, no doubt. She'd heard the rumors.

The young woman beamed. "I'd like a sweet tea, please." Her voice was kind.

Shannon glanced at Aiden and lifted a brow. "And a root beer float?"

"You know me." He winked. How many times had

she gotten lost in his sky-blue eyes?

"You two know each other?" His female companion piped up, as if she thought the situation was fascinating. It wasn't.

"This is my ex," Aiden volunteered.

The young woman's eyes widened and an unreadable expression crossed her face. "Shannon?" She reached for her hand. "Oh, I'm so sorry for your loss. Aiden told me."

She really fought back tears now. Was Aiden's girlfriend offering sympathy? Or was it pity? Perhaps she was referring to her losing Aiden and not her parents.

"I…it's okay." She shook off her emotional reaction, something she'd had to do a lot lately to stay strong for her siblings. "I'll get your drinks."

She hurried to the soda fountain after stopping to see if table seven needed anything.

"Will you help out the customer at the counter, please? I'm super busy right now," Shelby asked, as she passed carrying a large tray laden with several entrée platters.

"Sure." Anything to distract her from Aiden and his girlfriend.

She dropped off number three's drinks and took their order, with not so much as a glance in Aiden's direction, then hurried back to the waiting customer. She handed him a menu and he studied it. "Would you like anything to drink, sir?"

His head popped up from the menu and she stared at the most handsome face she'd ever laid eyes on. Oh, my. One look at this man made her forget Aiden even existed.

"Coffee, please." His smile was easy. And just as gorgeous as the rest of him.

She briefly glanced at his ring finger. Not that he would ever give her the time of day. "Coming right up."

"I take it black."

Yeah, a man as attractive and rugged as he was. She would have guessed he'd take it black. Not that coffee preference had anything to do with looks. But she could picture this man living in a cabin in the woods, sitting out on his porch as the sun rose, watching deer prance through the nearby woods to drink from the serene creek that meandered through his property. Surveying the land from atop a horse. Like one of those cute cowboys on the cover of the romance novels in Walmart.

She set his coffee in front of him, burying her wayward thoughts. "Are you ready to order now or should I come back?"

"No, now's fine." His eyes grazed the menu again, then

settled on her face. "What do you suggest, Shannon?"

She glanced down at her name badge. It wasn't often she got asked that question. And not usually with her name tacked on. In truth, she hadn't eaten at the restaurant much. Meals were half-price for employees, but it was still cheaper to bring a sandwich from home. "Um, the burgers are good. Unless you want an entrée. In that case, I'd recommend the chicken fried steak. I've never had it, but it seems to be popular with our customers."

"And why haven't *you* had it, if it's so popular?" His smile was teasing.

She shrugged. "I just…I don't eat here much."

"Hm…what does that say about the quality then?" Still teasing.

"No, it's not that. It's just…it's more economical to eat something from home."

He nodded. "I see. Well then, let me get two orders of chicken fried steak with…" He looked up at her. "Which sides do you recommend?"

"A baked potato and the steamed broccoli?" She raised her shoulders.

"Okay, then. A baked potato and the steamed broccoli."

Her brow rose. "Wait. You said *two*? Are you expecting someone?" She glanced toward the door.

"Uh, yeah, you can say that."

She should have guessed he had a date. "Okay, two chicken fried steaks with baked potato and steamed broccoli coming right up. Unless you need the second one to go?"

"Nope."

She quickly jotted Number 4 and his preferred sides down on her order pad. "It'll just be a little bit."

"Sounds good."

She dropped the order ticket off on the carousel so the kitchen staff could begin the customer's order. Two orders. That still puzzled her. But a man that good looking wouldn't be dining alone. He probably had women lined up out the door and around his cabin. He could certainly have his pick.

She made her rounds once again, filling drinks, serving orders, and cleaning off tables. She slipped a nice tip into her pocket. That would likely be gas for Walmart to go get Brighton's shoes later.

"Would you like a refill?" She carried the carafe of coffee back to the customer at the counter.

"Sure. Thanks, Shannon."

It felt a little strange the way he kept using her name. Like they knew each other or something. But she didn't know him. No, she'd *definitely* remember if she'd met Mr. Drop-Dead-Throw-Me-Down-And-Roll-Me-Over-Into-My-Grave Gorgeous.

Twenty minutes later, Aiden and his girlfriend neared the cash register. "Thanks for lunch. It was great."

She nodded and took Aiden's money. She placed the bills in the register, then handed back his change.

"Nah, keep it as a tip. You'll need it for those kiddos. Tell them hello for me."

She pressed her lips together, but managed a brief nod and a thank you for the tip. She sighed in relief as they finally left the restaurant.

The ding from the kitchen indicated the man at the counter's food was ready. She took both plates and placed them in front of him. She glanced around but didn't see the other diner he'd mentioned.

"Thank you," he said.

"Is your guest not coming then? I could box it up, if not," she offered.

"Uh, no. Actually, would *you* like to join me?"

Her heart flip flopped. She frowned. "Join you?"

"Are you…can you take a break right now?"

She looked toward the door and her area of the dining room. He was the only patron that remained in her section. The others had all cleared out. "I might be able to. But why?"

"I actually ordered this for you."

"Me? Why? I don't understand."

"Are you hungry?" He gestured to the seat next to

him. "Please, join me."

"Let me…let me just tell my coworker."

She hurried and notified Shelby that she was taking a break. She didn't mention the hot customer who'd asked her to eat with him. She quickly moved toward the restroom to wash her hands, then filled a glass with ice water and took it to where her lunchmate sat.

Her hands trembled slightly as she planted herself in the seat next to him.

"I'm Wesley, by the way." He extended his hand and she shook it.

"Nice to meet you."

He folded his hands together. "Mind if I pray?"

"No." She bowed her head and listened as he prayed out loud, thanking God for his food and his company. "Thanks for eating with me. Dining alone is no fun."

"You're welcome. Thanks for offering." She smiled, nearly pinching herself to make sure this wasn't a dream.

"My pleasure." He took his steak knife and a fork and cut through his chicken fried steak.

"Why did you buy an extra meal for me?"

He shrugged. "You said you'd never had the chicken fried steak. I thought you might like to try it."

His kindness caught her off-guard. "So, do you do that for every waitress you meet?"

"No. It's never happened before."

She took a sip of water. "Why me?"

"You looked like you could use a break."

"Well, you're right about that. Thanks again."

He nodded. "So, tell me about yourself, Shannon."

"What do you want to know?"

"Family? I thought I overheard that guy say something about kids? You married?"

"Uh, no. I take care of my younger siblings."

"Oh, okay. I see." He nodded. "And your parents?"

"They…they recently passed." It was still tough to say that without breaking down.

"Really? I'm sorry. I shouldn't have asked."

"No, it's okay. You didn't know."

His Adam's apple bobbed. "That must be hard."

"Yeah, it is. But I'd rather not talk about it."

He lifted his hands as though he were backing off. "Totally understand."

"You?" Her brow lifted. "Family?"

"Not married. No kids. I still live at home with my parents, believe it or not."

Her smiled widened. "No cabin in the woods?"

He rubbed the scruff on his face. "I guess I should've shaved this morning. I wasn't planning on meeting a pretty girl. I'm usually clean shaven."

He'd likely look gorgeous either way. But… Her

cheeks warmed. He thought she was pretty?

He glanced at his flannel shirt and chuckled. "No cabin. I wouldn't mind, though. That sounds nice."

"It does, doesn't it?"

He nodded. "So, do you live in the area?"

"Near Cross Plains. You?"

"I'm out between Holton and Nebraska."

"Oh, I think I remember something about a tornado ripping through there several years back."

"That's right. Wasn't there also one in Cross Plains just a couple of years ago?"

"Yeah. It hit one of our neighbor's properties, but no one was hurt that I know of. It also went through the hilltop area above Vevay, I heard. Touched down a few places there. Closer to Center Square, I believe."

"Oh, wow. Do y'all have a basement?"

"A small shelter. It's better than nothing, though. Do you?"

"Oh, yeah. My mom insisted on one before we even thought about purchasing a place. That was a priority. And good thing. We've used it several times."

She glanced down at her barely eaten meal. "I don't mind talking, but maybe we should try to eat before my break is over."

"Good idea." He grinned, then dug into his baked potato. "This is good."

She nodded and took a few bites. They ate in silence until they were both nearly finished.

"So, Cross Plains? My grandparents actually live out that way. They're in Pleasant Township, I believe."

"Really?"

He nodded. "What a coincidence."

"That's cool. So, do you visit them often?"

"Ah, every once in a while."

She set her silverware and napkin on top of her empty plate. "Okay, well you know what *my* job is. What do *you* do?"

"I'm a graphic designer. I design websites, signage, that sort of thing."

She frowned. "Really?"

He chuckled. "Is something wrong with what I said?"

"No, it's just…well, you don't look like you sit at a computer all day. I picture you doing something a little more…physical."

He briefly surveyed himself. "You noticed my muscles, huh?"

She likely turned all kinds of shades of red.

He laughed out loud. "I was joking."

She smiled timidly. "Of course, I noticed. Who wouldn't?" Yeah, she just said that out loud.

"I do work out at the gym. It's nice to know someone

actually noticed." He winked. "But, to be honest, I have worked on my dad's construction crew and still do from time to time. It's just not my field of choice."

Shelby waltzed by and tossed Shannon a pointed look. "Break's up, sweetie."

Shannon frowned and turned to Wesley. "Well, I guess that's my cue to get back to work."

"Ah, too bad. This was nice."

"Thank you for the meal. *That* was nice."

"It was my pleasure, Shannon. We'll have to do it again sometime. Maybe when you're not working?"

Had he just asked her on a date? Her heart sped up.

"I don't know. I don't get a lot of time to myself. I have the kids and…" she shrugged.

"That's not a problem. I'll just stop by here again then, if you don't mind. Are you working all week?"

"I pretty much work every day during the week while the kids are in school."

"Great. I'll be seeing you then." He nudged his head toward a customer. "I better let you get back to work."

She nodded, then grabbed a menu to take to the waiting diner, but she kept an eye on Wesley. He pulled his wallet out of his pocket and left a tip. That hadn't been necessary. Especially after he'd just purchased a meal for her. He moved to the register and Shelby rang up his bill.

She turned to the customer. "Would you like something to drink?"

"Sure. I'll take a Coke. And I'm ready to order right now."

She glanced over just as Wesley exited the restaurant. He lifted his hand to wave goodbye and she smiled and dipped her head in response.

"Sure, what would you like, sir?"

As Shannon finished up her work day, memories of her time spent with Wesley occupied her thoughts. He'd seemed like a really nice guy. Not only had he purchased her meal and kept her company, he'd also left a generous tip. She looked forward to him returning to the restaurant.

FIVE

Gorgeous. That's what she was.

Wesley could not get the blonde-haired, blue-eyed beauty out of his mind. What good fortune he had, having stumbled upon Shannon. She seemed to have such a pure heart. Selfless, apparently being the sole provider of her siblings. Hardworking. He'd seen how she'd bustled about the restaurant. She appeared to be overdue for a break when he'd walked in.

And he thought he'd just gone in because he was hungry. Well, he might have been hungry, but there was no doubt in his mind that meeting Shannon had been a Divine appointment.

Just like that, they'd clicked. He'd never had that with any woman in the past. Not that he had in mind to jump into a relationship with someone he'd barely met, but…

Whew. His senses were on overload.

But he needed to take a step back. There was so much he didn't know about her. Was she saved? Did she even go to church? He wished he had asked. But their brief time together had flown by.

Perhaps their next meeting would provide more information. Or...what if he caught her when she got off work? He did have his laptop in the truck. He could work right there and just wait in the parking lot until she walked to her car.

Wesley was deep into a project for a client, when a knock on the window of his truck startled him. He glanced up to see an officer standing next to his door. He frowned, then turned the key in the ignition to roll the window down.

"May I help you, officer?"

"Yes, sir. We've had a call about you."

"About *me*?"

"Are you stalking someone who works at this restaurant?"

"Me? Stalking? No. I mean, I *am* waiting for my friend. I'm not sure what time she gets off."

"If she's your *friend,* wouldn't you *know* what time

she gets off?" Wesley didn't appreciate the cop's cocky tone.

"I would go in and ask her, but I don't want to bother her."

"I see." The officer nodded. "Or you could just call her."

"I don't actually have her phone number."

"Why don't you Google it?"

He frowned. "I don't know her last name either."

He should have just kept his mouth shut. The cop didn't need to know what information he was privy to. Why had he even said that? It's not like it was this cop's business. Was he just setting him up? It sure seemed like it.

"*Friend*, huh? So, instead you're just waiting out in the parking lot all day? It sounds an awful lot like stalking to me."

"Wait a minute. You said someone called? From the restaurant?" Had Shannon reported him? He hoped that wasn't the case.

"I'm not permitted to say who the call came from. But I'm going to have to ask you to leave."

"Why?" Not that he meant to argue with the officer.

"We can discuss it in my patrol car if you'd prefer." The officer's piercing gaze meant business.

He lifted his hands. "I don't want any trouble. Okay,

I'll leave." He surrendered and turned over the ignition. *Sheesh!*

"Thank you. Have a nice day."

Yeah, right.

Wesley grumbled as he pulled out of the parking lot. *Now what?*

The officer followed close behind him until he headed out of town. Did the man think he'd turn around and go back to the restaurant? He was surely tempted to. It was a free country, wasn't it?

But what if Shannon *had* been the one who'd called? Did *she* think he was stalking her? He sincerely hoped not. Perhaps returning to the restaurant wasn't such a great idea after all. But he'd been so sure that God had arranged their meeting. Maybe he'd been wrong.

He'd likely scared her off by being so forward. *Way to go, Wes.*

SIX

Shannon pulled her car into the driveway, half excited about her day and meeting gorgeous Wesley and half nervous about Melanie's well-being.

She needed to pick her baby sister up from the neighbors as soon as possible. The babysitter never did call her. She hoped it was a good thing. No news was good news, right?

How she'd hated leaving her with a virtual stranger. But what could she do? If she didn't work, she couldn't put food on the table. She'd have to do an internet search on what the cheapest foods to eat were and plan their meals around that.

With Christmas just around the corner, she *really* needed to stretch her dollars. Maybe she'd also look up affordable Christmas gifts or fun things to do without spending a lot of money. A borrowed Christmas movie or two from the library would be a nice treat for them. Popcorn was a luxury, but at least it was cheap. She could buy a box of the microwave kind next time she was at the dollar store.

She truly wanted to make the best of this Christmas for the kids. A fresh tree was out of the question, but maybe she could find an artificial one at the thrift store. They already had lights and ornaments up in the attic, so she wouldn't have to buy those.

Before heading to the neighbors' place, she hurried into her house and dropped off her purse. She'd stuffed some money into her pocket to pay the babysitter, although they hadn't discussed a price. She'd been scurrying just to get Melanie taken care of, that she'd left without even thinking of payment.

Shannon put her ear close to the crack in the neighbors' door to see if she could hear any crying. She didn't, but that didn't necessarily mean anything. After knocking on the door twice, it finally opened to her.

The teen girl, Avery, greeted her with a smile. "She did fine. Only cried for about ten or twenty minutes after you left."

"Twenty minutes?"

"I found a toy for her, but that didn't work, so I turned the tv on. She loves tv."

Great, so her baby sister sat in front of the television all day long? Shannon nodded, but frowned. She shouldn't assume the worst. It wasn't fair to the babysitter.

"I took her outside too and pushed her on the swing."

"The swing?" Her heart raced. She pictured Melanie letting go of the ropes and flipping onto the ground. *Just stop!*

"Don't worry, it's a kiddie swing. Trust me. Really, she did fine."

Shannon's eyes roamed the room, but Melanie was nowhere in sight. She wouldn't panic. "Where is she?"

"Oh, she's napping in my sister's room. I'll go get her." Avery disappeared around a corner, then came back a moment later with Melanie in her arms. "Look who's here," she said in a baby voice.

Melanie burst into tears the moment she spotted Shannon. She held out her arms and Shannon took her from Avery.

"It's okay, baby." She jostled Melanie on her hip. "How much do I owe you?"

"Can you swing twenty-five? I've gotta put gas in my car."

"Sure. That sounds good." Twenty-five bucks was a steal. Maybe she should consider using Avery more often. That would be one way she could save money. She dug into her pocket with her free hand and handed a twenty and a five-dollar bill to Avery.

"Thanks." Avery stuffed the money in her pants pocket and handed Melanie's bag to Shannon.

"No, thank you. You were a life saver." She headed toward the door. She couldn't wait to get home and relax for a few moments before the bus arrived with the boys. "You're sure she did fine?"

"Honest. After that first crying fit, she did great."

Shannon sighed and nodded to the door. Yeah, she'd been overreacting. "Do you mind if I use you again?"

"Anytime. As long as I'm home and don't have plans. I could use some extra cash. She'll probably cry less once she gets used to me." Avery smiled and waved as they walked out. "Bye, Mel."

"Bye-bye!" Melanie waved with her chubby little hand. She seemed content.

Shannon walked the short distance to their home. "Look at you. Not a tear. I think you're just trying to make sister worry, aren't you?"

"Momma!" Melanie smacked Shannon's cheek with a kiss.

"I'm not Momma, baby. But you probably won't remember much of Momma when you grow up, will you?"

"No. Momma go bye-bye." Melanie likely didn't even realize what she was saying. "Going home?"

46

"Yep, we're going home. Did you have a good time with Avery? Was she nice to you?"

"A, B, C, D…" Melanie sang.

"That was good! Did you learn that today? Did Avery teach you that?"

"No, frog."

"A frog?"

"Yep. Frog say A, B, C, D…" she let off humming, probably not remembering how the rest went.

"Was it E, F, G?"

"Yep. E, F, G."

"Very good, sweetheart. I think you might have had a good time at Avery's."

"Yep. Had good time."

Good. That made her feel much better about leaving Melanie with their teen neighbor. Although Shannon was only a year older than Avery, her responsibilities had aged her. Emotionally, she was closer to a decade older.

She brought out a few toys for Melanie, then loafed on the couch for about ten minutes, pondering her day. All things considered, it had actually been a good day so far.

Now, to figure out what she'd make for dinner. The boys would be returning home from school anytime. Since Jaycee was only in kindergarten that let out around noon, he stayed in an afternoon program until he could ride the school bus home with Brighton. It seemed to work out well and allowed her to work a couple of much-needed extra hours.

She thought again about the pleasant lunch she'd shared with handsome Wesley. She hoped she hadn't been dreaming, because if she had, she'd rather not wake up. He'd seemed so kind and genuine. She couldn't wait for the day he'd walk back into the restaurant.

SEVEN

"Shannon! Someone's here!" Brighton hollered from the front room.

Shannon set the basket of laundry down on the bed and walked into the living room. "Did they knock?"

"Yeah."

"Did you look out the window? Who is it?" Shannon hated opening the door to strangers. Since it was just her and her siblings, she was now the adult-in-charge. But she didn't always feel like an adult.

Brighton shrugged. "I don't know. Some old people."

"Elderly people," she corrected. "*Old* sounds rude."

"Whatever."

"Not whatever. *Okay* or *yes, ma'am* would be appropriate."

"Whatever."

She pinned him with a warning stare. "Brighton."

"Okay." He lifted his hands. "You're sounding like Dad now."

She went to the door and looked through the peep hole. *Hm...was it the Amish man they'd seen at Walmart the other day?*

She opened the door a few inches, but kept her foot firmly behind it. Not that her foot would prevent anyone from barging in if they wished. "May I help you?"

The man spoke, "My name is Christopher and this is my wife, Judy. I met Jaycee at the store the other day."

Shannon nodded, a tentative smile on her face. "I thought it was you. How did you know where we lived?"

"I mentioned your situation to some of my neighbors and it turns out one of them knew your folks."

"Oh." She swallowed, not wanting to dwell on her parents' death.

"Well, Jaycee had mentioned that you lost your folks. Judy and I, we'd like to help you."

Judy stepped forward. Two loaves of bread were in her hands, and she had something tucked under her arms. "We brought you some bread that I baked this morning. And jam."

"And cookies!" Christopher said, holding up a plastic bag.

Tears welled in Shannon's eyes at their kindness and

generosity. "Thank you so much. That's so thoughtful of you."

Amish people weren't dangerous, were they? They sure didn't seem like it. At least, not this older couple on her doorstep. Should she invite them inside? She didn't know, but she didn't want to be rude. Mom would've invited them in. "Would you…would you like to come in?"

The older couple shared a tender look. "Sure, but just for a few moments," Christopher said.

"I'm sure you're busy," Judy interjected.

"It's okay. Come in." She moved to the side so they could enter. "You may have a seat." She gestured toward the couch.

One thing Shannon had always loved about their house is that it felt light and airy. With lots of windows and light-colored walls, their home felt welcoming.

"Brighton, go bring the others in." Shannon turned to their guests. "Would you like some water?"

"Sure, I'll take some," Judy said, handing the loaves to Shannon.

"Me, too," Christopher added.

Shannon quickly took the loaves of bread and jam Judy offered to the kitchen, and filled two glasses with filtered water. As she walked back into the living room, the children also did.

"Look, Melanie! It's Santa!" Jaycee shrieked and raced toward their Amish guests.

Shannon laughed. "This is Christopher and his wife, Judy. It's not Santa, Jaycee."

"He looks like Santa to me. He even bought me a candy bar!" Jaycee carefully studied Christopher, who sat sharing a large grin with his wife.

"I brought you cookies today," Christopher's smiled broadened.

"Cookie!" Melanie squealed.

Shannon stepped forward and pulled Melanie by the hand. "Judy and Christopher, I'd like you to meet Brighton, Jaycee, and Melanie. And I'm Shannon."

"*Gut* to meet you." The couple's heads bobbed.

"Won't you have a cookie?" Christopher held out the bag to Shannon.

She smiled her appreciation, then took it and distributed one to each of the children. "Go sit at the table so you don't make a mess," she told her siblings.

"Thanks, Santa!" Jaycee grinned and immediately took a bite out of his delicacy before reaching the table.

Shannon pointed Jaycee to the his designated dining chair and shook her head. "I guess we're going to have a hard time convincing him. Especially since you brought cookies."

Christopher winked. "I don't mind."

"It was kind of you to come by." Shannon bit into the most delicious sugar cookie she'd ever tasted. "This is wonderful!"

"I can teach you how to make them, if you'd like," Judy offered.

"That would be great. But I'm afraid I don't have the ingredients on hand. I don't do much baking."

"You and the *kinner* could come to our house. We can make them there." Judy nodded.

"Where do you live?"

"Pleasant Township. Off the Two-fifty. Not too far," Christopher said. "I'm sure the little ones would like to see our new kittens. And the foal that was just born last week."

"You have a horse?" Brighton joined in the conversation.

"He's got reindeer too!" Jaycee had wasted no time gobbling down his delicacy.

Christopher chuckled. "I suppose there might be some deer out in our woods."

"See? I told you!" Jaycee now stood next to Christopher, patting his hand.

"That sounds like it would be fun. What do you guys think? Do you want to go visit Christopher and Judy one of these days?" As soon as Melanie finished, Shannon helped her down from the dining chair and cleaned the crumbs off her hands.

"And we get to bring more cookies home?" Brighton asked.

"Yep. Whatever Shannon makes she can take home." Judy took little Melanie onto her lap.

"Cool! When are we going, Shan?" Brighton smiled.

"I don't know." She turned to Christopher and Judy. "When is a good time for you?"

"How about Saturday?" Christopher looked to his wife and she nodded.

"I think that would work well for us." Shannon sat on Mom's rocking chair.

"Great. Then Saturday it is. I'll write down the address for you. Come whenever it's convenient. We should be home all day." Christopher seemed as excited as Jaycee was.

"Thank you. That sounds wonderful."

"We will have a *gut* time," Judy said, stroking Melanie's back.

Shannon was a little surprised at how well Melanie had taken to the couple. She seemed perfectly content to sit with Judy.

A half hour later, they said goodbye to their unexpected but very welcomed guests. Shannon found herself looking forward to Saturday.

EIGHT

Shannon frowned as she punched her timecard to clock out of work on Friday afternoon. Disappointment darkened her mood on the drive home.

Wesley hadn't come back. He'd said he would, but he didn't.

She sighed. Didn't anyone keep their word nowadays? He seemed to be genuine when he said it. Had the attraction only been one-sided? Apparently so.

But maybe she should give him the benefit of the doubt. After all, he *had* bought her a meal. Maybe something terrible had happened. No, she wouldn't think that way. She'd rather he be unreliable than in a hospital somewhere. She'd had enough tragedy to last a lifetime.

Perhaps he'd gotten busy and he'd show up next week. Yeah, she'd cling to that hope. Because clinging to hope was better than assuming the worst or having no hope at all.

A relationship at this point in time probably wasn't the best idea anyway. She didn't have time to date. She had a household to run, bills to pay, mouths to feed, shoes to buy.

And the Christmas gifts. She still had no idea what she'd be able to afford to get the kids. It would be difficult enough trying to keep her spirits up without their parents there. How would her siblings react to their first Christmas without Mom and Dad?

She already knew how *she* was feeling. Lost. Empty. Alone. And missing Mom and Dad with every breath she took.

It would likely be the worst Christmas they'd ever experienced. Her heart ached at the thought.

"Shan! Shannon! Come on. Let's go! Let's go!" Jaycee bounced up and down on Shannon's bed, waking her out of dreams that were too impossible to ever come true.

"Really, Jaycee? What time is it?" She rubbed the sleepiness from her eyes and squinted at the alarm clock.

"It's seven! Santa said we could come at any time. Come on, let's go!"

"Seven, Jaycee? It's Saturday. Let me sleep in." She yawned. She hadn't fallen asleep until well after midnight, researching Christmas on the cheap.

"Too late! Mel's up."

"Jay. Cee." She employed her best warning tone.

"I didn't wake her up, promise."

"Fine. Let me get dressed, then I'll figure out breakfast."

"Bright and me already had cereal."

"It's Brighton and I. And I hope you only took one bowl each. It has to last us." She hated that she sounded like an old miser.

"We did. We're saving room for cookies!"

"Cereal and cookies, huh?" *I must be the worst substitution for a mother. Ever.* "You should eat a piece of fruit too." It was the mature thing to say, wasn't it?

"Ah, Shan," he whined.

"I mean it. If you want to have cookies at Judy and Christopher's, you need to have some fruit." Of course, knowing Jaycee, he'd find a way to sneak a cookie anyhow.

"Can I share a banana with Bright or Mel?

"It's *may I*, and yes, that will be fine."

She watched as Jaycee skipped from her bedroom. Well, time to begin the day whether she was ready or not. At least it promised to be interesting.

Wesley veered off the dirt road and pulled into the back entrance of his grandparents' property. They'd requested he do that each time he came so his truck wouldn't be visible from the road. He'd honored their wishes without argument.

As he neared the barn, he noticed activity in the yard. Did his grandparents have company?

He parked and slipped his keys into his pocket and sauntered toward the house. If Grandpa was busy, he'd wait to go see him. Perhaps Grandma was baking something delicious. Spending time with his grandparents had always been a pleasure, especially when Grandma had fresh baked treats for him.

He pulled the screen door open and it groaned in protest. "Grandma? You in here?"

"In the kitchen, dear." He heard muffled voices.

His grin widened. His favorite place.

He waltzed to the kitchen prepared to pull his grandmother into a hug. Sweetness assaulted his senses the moment he stepped into the room.

Grandma turned around along with her guest. They both wore aprons tainted with flour. "Wesley!"

His eyes widened as he laid his eyes on the girl of his dreams. Right there. In his grandmother's kitchen. Looking as attractive as ever. Was he dreaming all this up?

"Are you stalking me?" Shannon pointed a finger at him, an unreadable expression on her face.

No, he wasn't dreaming. This had just turned into a nightmare. Great, now she would *really* think he was some creep. And she'd likely blame him for roping his grandparents into his scheme.

"I promise." He held up his hands. "I'm not stalking you. I had no idea you were even here."

Her lips moved slightly upward. Did she believe him or not? He couldn't tell.

He frowned. "You're not going to call the police again, are you?"

"The police?" Shannon and Grandma both said it at the same time.

"Yeah, like at the restaurant the other day."

A strange look flickered across Shannon's face. "What are you talking about?"

"The police. At the restaurant. When you called and told them I was stalking you. Does that ring a bell?"

"I have absolutely no idea what you're talking about. When you were at the restaurant, there were no police there."

"So it wasn't you?" Relief filled him.

"*What* wasn't me?"

"You didn't ask the police to run me out of the parking lot?"

She gasped. "No. Why would I do that?"

"Well, someone did."

"What?" She shook her head. "Okay, wait. Start over from the beginning. I am *so* confused."

"So am I," Grandma said. "I'm guessing you two have met before, then?"

"Yes," they both said.

"Okay," Wesley began. "The other day when we met at the restaurant, after we had lunch—"

"You two had lunch together?" Grandma's eyes widened.

"Yes," they both answered again. This time a smile played on her lips.

"After I left the restaurant," he continued, "I decided to just wait in my truck until you got off work. So we could talk."

"You did?" Shannon seemed surprised.

"Yes. But then a police officer pulled up and asked me to leave. Or, really, he ran me off. He said someone from the restaurant had called and reported a stalker. I thought it was you."

"It wasn't me." She shook her head. "I had no idea. I was expecting you to come back during the week like you said you were going to."

"I had planned to." He shrugged. "But I figured that if you called the cops on me, you definitely didn't want me coming back."

"Was I rude to you?"

"Rude? No, of course not. You were sweet."

Her countenance softened along with her voice. "Then why would you think it was *me* who called the police?"

"I don't know. You were the only one I talked to. Who else would it have been?"

Her shoulders lifted. "I have no idea. I'll have to ask when I go into work next week."

"So, does this mean you *don't* mind if I stop by to see you?" He couldn't tamper the hopefulness in his tone.

"I already told you that I'd like that." She sounded shy now. "By the way, thanks for the nice tip. You really didn't have to do that."

His gaze caressed her beautiful face. "I wanted to." He stepped close and boldly reached for her hand.

A throat cleared loudly, reminding him that he and Shannon weren't alone in the room. He backed away, feeling deprived of the physical contact they'd almost had. "Sorry, Grandma."

A timer went off.

"Sounds like the first batch of cookies is done." Grandma opened the door of the oven compartment of the woodstove and pulled out a cookie sheet. She looked to Shannon. "You'll need to slide these onto the cooling rack."

She broke eye contact with him and moved to retrieve a spatula and potholder from the counter.

Wesley stepped out of the way, into the kitchen's entryway. "I think I might hear a baby crying?"

"Oh, that's Melanie. I'll get her in just a little bit."

He neared and held out his hand for the spatula. "I'll do this, if you'd like. You can go get her."

The shyness was back. "Thank you."

He stared after her as she disappeared from the room. He blew out a breath, shaking his head. He still couldn't get over the fact that Shannon was *here*. In his grandparents' home. What good fortune he'd stumbled upon! Wait, good fortune? No, it wasn't that at all. His first instinct had been correct. God had planned their initial meeting. And now, it seemed, He'd arranged for them to meet again in the most unlikely place he would have imagined. And if it *was* God, well…

"I see someone has taken a liking to our *Englisch* guest." Grandma's words broke his inner musings. Or, more accurate, the love spell.

"How do you know Shannon?"

She handed him a cookie. "It's quite a story. But I think maybe she'd like to share it with you."

His expression puzzled. It wasn't like Grandma to give up a chance to tell a story. "Do you like her, Grandma?"

"I do."

Their conversation ceased and silence filled the room as soon as Shannon walked back in carrying an adorable little girl, whose face appeared to be a much younger version of Shannon's. "This is my baby sister, Melanie. Melanie, meet Wesley."

The little one took one look at him and clung to Shannon with all her might.

He chuckled. "Wow. Glad to know I have such a magnetic personality."

"*Jah*, but it looks like you need to turn the magnet over," Grandma jested.

"It's okay." Shannon jostled the little one. "Wesley is a nice man. Judy is his grandma."

"Judy!" Melanie squealed and reached out to his grandmother.

"She loves your grandma."

He loved the giggle that tripped from Shannon's lips. But he really shouldn't be noticing her lips.

"I see that."

"Your grandparents invited us over to make cookies and see their farm. The boys are outside with your grandpa."

Grandma approached the table with Melanie on her hip. The little one's face beamed as she bit into her cookie. "Why don't you two go find your *grossdawdi* before Melanie and I decide we want all these cookies for ourselves." She winked.

"Sure thing, Grandma." He winked back. He turned to Shannon and cocked his head sideways, gesturing toward the door.

She followed him outside. "Okay, I have so many questions for you right now," she blurted out the moment they stepped out the door.

He laughed. "Yeah, me too. How on earth do you know my grandparents and why have I never met you before? Oh, wait, I'm sorry. Ladies, first."

"No, it's okay. We actually met your grandparents at Walmart. Well, Jaycee did."

"Jaycee?"

"My youngest brother. He's five," she explained.

"Walmart?" His brow arched. "Really?"

"Yeah. Then they showed up at our front door the other day bearing gifts." Her grin expanded.

"That's interesting."

Grandpa approached with a boy on either side of him. The youngest one held Grandpa's hand, but clung to a kitten with the other.

Shannon stepped close to him and whispered, "That's Jaycee. He thinks your grandpa is Santa Claus." Her hot breath on his ear did strange things to his insides.

He glanced at her, a smile dancing on his lips. "Really?"

"Shan, look what Santa's got! I bet lots of little boys and girls want kittens this year. That's why he has so many." He raced to his sister and held up a kitten. "Want to hold her? Santa said I could take her home if it's okay with you."

"No, Jaycee. No animals. Sorry," Shannon said.

"Ah, for reals? But Santa said…" Jaycee looked up at Grandpa, his eyes pleading.

"I said *if* your sister said *yes*. But that's okay, I won't give them all away. I'll keep one here so you can play with her when you come over."

"You will?" Jaycee crushed Grandpa's legs with a bear hug. "Thank you, Santa!"

"Jaycee, it's Christopher." Shannon sighed.

Grandpa chuckled. "I don't think anyone is going to convince him otherwise."

"Grandma said to tell you that cookies are ready," Wesley interjected while he had the chance.

"That's what we were just going to check on," Grandpa said, his eyes sparkling. It looked like he was having just as good of a time as the boys were.

"Perfect timing." The older boy rubbed his hands together.

"You boys make sure to wash your hands before you

take any cookies," Shannon insisted. She sounded like she took her mothering responsibilities seriously. Which made Wesley admire her even more.

Grandpa led his charges into the house and held the door open for the two of them.

Wesley looked at his grandfather. "We'll be inside in just a minute."

Grandpa's brow shot up, then he nodded.

He reached for her hand and pulled her toward the porch swing. "Let's talk?" He released her.

"Sure." Her smile was easy.

They both sat down. "You said you had questions?"

"Yeah. Your grandparents are Amish."

"Very observant of you," he teased.

"But you're not."

"Nope. Never have been."

"Explain that to me."

"Well, Dad left the Amish community when he was a young man. Since he was already baptized into the church, he was excommunicated."

"I'm sorry, I'm not that familiar with Amish culture. What does that mean exactly?"

"Grandpa and Grandma can't have fellowship with him, per the Amish rules."

"But they're okay with you?"

"My grandparents are, yeah. But not everyone in

their community likes it when I come to visit. That's why Grandpa asked me to park in back. It causes them less grief."

"Oh." She frowned. "That's kind of sad."

"Yeah. Dad would like to visit with his parents, but they're not allowed to."

"Why do you suppose that is? I mean, aren't they free to choose who they want to spend time with?"

"No, not really. The Amish culture has a lot of good things going for it, but freedom is not one of them. They are bound by manmade rules. That's one of the reasons Dad left. He didn't think it was right to have to live under a bunch of rules that had no true Biblical basis."

"Half of that went right over my head." She laughed. "Biblical basis?"

"From the Bible. For example, the Bible doesn't speak of only owning a horse and buggy, but it is something their district insists on. They're allowed to ride in cars, but not allowed to own them. And that's just one of the many things they teach that isn't Biblical."

"Is that why they dress the way they do? Because they have to?"

"Yep." He stared at her. "Do you mind if I ask you something?"

"Go ahead."

"How old are you?"

"Eighteen. How old are you?"

"Twenty-three."

"And you said you still live with your parents?"

"Yeah. They haven't kicked me out yet, and I can save a lot more money by not having to pay rent. Although I do contribute some money to the family budget." He grinned. "When I decide to settle down, I should have plenty of money for a nice down payment on a piece of property." Why had he said that? He hoped she didn't think he was hinting at anything. Because he wasn't.

"That's great." She shrugged. "I don't know what my plans are. I guess I have none. Now that I'm responsible for my siblings, I just have to care for them." Her voice wobbled and twin tears slid down her cheek.

"Hey." He slipped his arm around her shoulders. "It's okay."

She pushed the tears away. "I'm sorry. I don't mean to get emotional. It's just that every time I think that Mom and Dad are gone and they're not coming back…" More moisture gathered and poured down her face.

He gathered her close and let her cry. Had she even had a chance to grieve her parents' deaths? It seemed not.

She pulled back and he removed his arm from her shoulders. "I hate crying on you."

"It's all right. That's what friends are for. You may cry on me anytime."

She stared at him with her slightly red-rimmed eyes. "Friends?"

"Well, honestly, I'd like to be more than friends with you. But I'm not sure we're at that point in our relationship just yet."

"You would?"

"Very much so."

She smiled. "Me too."

"That's the best news I've heard all day. Second only to arriving at my grandparents' house and discovering that you were here." He glanced down at her hand. "Do you mind?"

The shy smile was back and she shook her head.

He reached for her hand with his and intertwined their fingers. "Tell me about yourself and your family."

She shrugged. "There's not really much to share."

"What was your life like growing up? When your parents were alive. If it's not too difficult to talk about."

"No, it's fine." She sighed. "I just graduated over the summer. This year was Jaycee's first year of kindergarten. Brighton's in sixth grade. Melanie's almost two."

"Wow, sounds like you all are pretty spread out."

She nodded. "We are. Seven years between Brighton and me, six years between Brighton and Jaycee, and three years between Jaycee and Mel. Melanie and I are over sixteen years apart. Do you have siblings?"

"It's just my younger brother and me. He's off at college right now. He'll be visiting for Christmas, though." His thumb slid over the top of her hand. "Do you attend church anywhere?"

"No. We occasionally went for holidays and such, but not every Sunday. But my parents were still good people."

"I have no doubt about that." But were they saved? He'd wanted to say the words aloud, but she might not be ready for that conversation. Especially considering her emotional state. He'd wait for the Lord's prompting. "Would you be interested in coming to church with me?"

Her eyes widened. She apparently hadn't expected that question. "Oh. Well, um, yeah, sure, I guess. Me and the kids?"

"Yes, definitely the kids too. I think they'll enjoy it."

She seemed to be thinking. "What…is there like a certain dress code?"

"No, not really. I mean, my mom always wanted us to dress in our best clothes for church to show respect for God's house. But that doesn't mean we dress fancy or anything. I usually just wear nice slacks and a button up shirt or a polo."

"Should I wear a dress?"

He'd love to see her in a dress. "You could if you want. Some women do, some don't."

"Okay."

"So, tomorrow? Or is that too soon?"

She grimaced. "I might have to wash a load of laundry tonight, but I think we can probably manage. What time do we need to be there?"

"I could pick you up at nine fifteen. Unless you don't want to attend Sunday school. In that case, I'd pick you up at ten fifteen."

"I think we can swing nine fifteen. The kids are used to getting up early for school."

"We usually go out to eat afterwards for lunch."

She frowned. "The kids and I can eat at home."

"I want you to come with us." He squeezed her hand. "And I wouldn't dream of letting you pay for it."

"Are you sure?"

"One hundred percent."

"It would be a nice treat for the kids. They haven't been out since…" She let the words fall off, but he caught their meaning.

"Well, then I'd love to treat them. And you."

She shook her head. "Thank you, Wesley. You're too sweet."

"It's truly my pleasure. I'm looking forward to it."

He pulled his phone out of his pocket. "Let me give you my phone number in case you need to get ahold of me for any reason."

"My phone's in my purse in the house."

"Well, then, how about if I send you a quick text? You can just save my contact info when you check it."

"Sure." She recited her phone number.

He quickly typed it into his keypad, then sent her a text message. "Great."

NINE

Shannon could scarcely wrap her mind around the turn of events. First, meeting Wesley at the restaurant. Next, Christopher and Judy randomly showing up on their doorstep. Then, being disappointed because Wesley hadn't returned to the restaurant, assuming he was probably a jerk. And now, she finds out that Wesley—*gorgeous* Wesley—is this sweet Amish couple's grandson?

Not only that, but he liked her. He *like liked* her. Like a lot. Enough to make future plans. Okay, it was just church, but still. This had to be one of the most amazing days of her life. She felt like she'd been slapped with the happy stick. She couldn't seem to erase the smile off her face.

They all sat around Judy and Christopher's table, enjoying the grilled chicken the men had prepared along with Judy's noodles, coleslaw, applesauce, pickles, and bread with what they'd called 'peanut butter spread.' Shannon sat across the table from Wesley, with Melanie between her and Judy. The boys sat on each side of Wesley, on a long wooden bench. Jaycee had insisted on sitting next to Christopher, or "Santa."

"We might have spotted a couple of deer out in the woods," Christopher said, sharing a knowing look with Jaycee. Was he encouraging this Santa charade? The stinker.

"I bet it was the reindeers!" Jaycee beamed.

Shannon held her tongue, although tempted to correct his speech. She looked at Wesley, whose smile broadened. He winked at her and she grinned back.

"Christopher and I have been talking." Judy pinned her gaze on Shannon. "How would you feel about us watching the little one for you while the other *kinner* are at school?"

Shannon's jaw nearly dropped. What a perfect solution! "Well, I could use an extra babysitter every now and then. What would you charge?"

"Oh, no, we wouldn't charge you a thing. It would be a blessing to have this *boppli* with us. Haven't had one in our home in a long time." She and Christopher shared a sad smile, briefly glancing at Wesley. No doubt, this family had experienced its own heartaches.

She fought back tears. Really? Seriously? They were offering to watch Melanie? For free? "I-I don't know what to say. That's such a kind offer."

"The way that little one takes to you, you'd think she's our *grossboppli*," Christopher said, studying his wife.

"Not just this one," Judy nodded to the boys.

"Sounds like a great opportunity for both of you." Wesley glanced at Shannon again, lifting his brow.

"Ah, I wanna come too! Can I skip school, Shan? Pleeaase?" Jaycee whined.

"If your little *schweschder's* here, I suspect Shannon will be bringing you and Brighton over when she picks her up. Ain't so?" Christopher looked to Shannon.

"Yes. I can bring the boys when I pick her up." But she felt like a charity case. Who was she kidding? She *was* a charity case. In this instance, she'd accept it. She had a feeling Christopher and Judy would be devastated if she refused their kind-hearted offer. She wouldn't have the heart to say no, even if she wanted to.

"And Judy just *might* have some treats waiting." Christopher winked at the boys.

"But you've got to do your best in school," Judy added.

"We will! Won't we, Brighton?" Jaycee's excitement was almost tangible.

Shannon didn't know what to say…or do. Her heart was so full right now. She couldn't wipe the smile off her face if she tried. Had she stepped into a fairy tale? Someone else's life? Because this was way beyond her blessing zone. At any moment, she feared she might wake up from this magnificent dream.

She stood from the table, with plate in hand.

Wesley shook his head attempting to communicate…*what*?

Christopher cleared his throat and bowed his head. Judy did likewise. Wesley also did, but only after shooting a wink in her direction. She had no idea Amish people prayed before *and* after every meal. Not that she'd ever been around any before now. She quickly sat back down and bowed her head as well.

Grandpa, Grandma, and Wesley escorted the Parker family to their vehicle. Wesley should be leaving now too, if he wanted to follow Shannon to her destination. He needed to know where they lived if he planned to pick them up in the morning for church.

"Do we have to go home now?" Jaycee whined as they approached her car.

"Yes. I still have things to do today," Shannon insisted.

"Like what?" He challenged.

"Laundry, for one. And I need to make dinner." She opened the door so Jaycee could climb into his booster in the backseat.

"But we can eat dinner here," he protested.

"No, we can't. Christopher and Judy have already been kind enough to feed us lunch. It would be rude to stay for dinner too. You want them to invite us back over, don't you?" She'd lowered her voice, but her words could still be clearly understood from just behind her, where Wesley stood. He averted his gaze, trying not to notice how nicely her jeans fit.

"Fine, we can go home. When can we come back?"

"Jaycee, we don't want to wear out our welcome. If we come over too much, they might not want us to come back."

"Shannon." The boy huffed in exasperation. "Don't you know that Santa loves kids and he *never* gets tired of them?"

Shannon turned around and Wesley caught her giggle. She closed the car door. "I tell you, that boy…" She shook her head.

"I see who provides all the entertainment at your house." Wesley grinned.

She rolled her eyes. "If you only knew."

Grandma stepped up to the other side of the vehicle, leading little Melanie by the hand. Shannon picked the little one up and placed her into her car seat, then fastened the straps.

"I'm planning to follow you home so I know where to pick you up tomorrow. If that's okay," Wesley said.

"Just so long as you're not stalking me." Shannon's teasing smile sent his pulse racing.

"Not stalking, I promise." He held up his arms in surrender and chuckled.

He caught her gaze resting on his biceps, then noticed a sudden blush on her cheeks.

She averted her eyes and cleared her throat. "Okay, then. I guess I'll see you…tomorrow…or were you planning to stay at the house a little while?"

He nodded. "Tomorrow. You said you had things to do, and I wouldn't want to spring myself on you unawares. I know my mom hates when people show up without prior notice. She likes to tidy up the house before guests come over."

"I totally get that. It's nice to have a heads-up. But I don't mind so much."

"I can maybe stop in when I drop you off after lunch tomorrow, if that works for you."

"That sounds perfect." She broke eye contact, then turned to his grandparents. "Thank you both so much for everything. The kids had a wonderful time."

"I suspect it wasn't just the kids." Grandpa chuckled. His joyful gaze moved from Shannon to Wesley.

"No, I did too," she admitted, casting an all-too-brief glance in his direction.

"If you'd like to drop Melanie off Monday morning, we'll be here," Grandma offered.

"That's so kind. I'll need to call my original babysitter, so right now it's a tentative yes. Should I call you?"

"That's not necessary, but we will take down your phone number in case we need to call you. And I can give you the number to the shanty." Grandma looked at Grandpa, who must've instinctively known what she was thinking. He hustled into the house and returned in short order with a pen and paper.

Shannon's brow shot up. "Shanty?"

Wesley chuckled. "They don't have a telephone inside the house. Instead, there is a phone booth of sorts that is shared by several families in the area. It's down the road. So, if you call, you'll need to leave a message. But beware that *everyone* who uses the phone will have access to the messages you leave. And if no one checks the messages, you may be waiting a while to hear back."

"Oh. Okay."

"It might not be the best idea to mention anything about babysitting in a message. Some of the members can get up in arms about things. Right, Grandpa?"

He nodded, but Wesley got the message that Grandpa didn't want to drag her into the community's goings-on. "Best not to mention it."

Shannon's look conveyed that she didn't know whether he meant best not to mention the members' testiness or if he was referring to babysitting.

"A short message like, 'This is Wesley. Please call me,' is usually what I leave. That way, nobody else has to know anything," Wesley clarified.

"Okay, that's what I'll do then if I need to get ahold of you. I better get going now. I hear the kids complaining already." She smiled again at Grandma and Grandpa.

How he loved her smile. He could just stand there all day and stare at her.

Grandpa chuckled. "I never liked to sit still when I was a *bu* either."

"When you were a *bu*?" Grandma's brow rose. "You can't sit still now."

"I suppose you're right, *fraa*."

Wesley loved it when his grandparents teased each other. They'd always seemed to have a strong relationship. It was just too bad it wasn't one they could share with Wesley's father.

TEN

Shannon's heart did a little flip when Wesley's truck pulled up behind her car in the driveway. Now he knew where she lived. Of course, if he intended to give them a ride to church tomorrow morning, it only stood to reason that he would need to know.

She stepped out of the car, handing the keys to Brighton so he could unlock the front door. He and Jaycee would let themselves in while she removed Melanie from her car seat.

Wesley approached. "Need any help?"

"No. I just need to take Melanie and put her down for her nap."

He nodded, looking unsure of what his next course of action should be.

"Like I said before, you're more than welcome to come in," she offered.

"Nah, I should let you go." He frowned. "I did kind

of want to ask you something first, though."

She rubbed Melanie's back, so she'd stay sleeping. "Do you mind holding on a minute? I'll be right back. Let me just put Mel down real quick."

"Sure. That's not a problem."

"You're welcome to take a seat on the porch." She said before disappearing into the house with her baby sister. She hurried to Melanie's room and laid her down in her toddler bed, kissing her soft little chubby cheek. "Sleep well, baby."

She hurried toward the door, but turned to Brighton before stepping out. "I'm going to talk to Wesley for just a little bit. Will you make sure no one gets into mischief, please?"

He held up his hands. "I'm not making any promises."

Shannon shot her best "you'd better do what I asked" look at Brighton.

"Fine." He shook his head. "Go outside and smooch with your boyfriend."

"Brighton." Her tone held warning. "You know Wesley is not my boyfriend." Yet.

"Uh huh."

Shannon ignored her brother and stepped out the door, determined not to make Wesley wait any longer than necessary. "Sorry about that."

"It's no problem."

She sat on one of the lawn chairs opposite Wesley.

"I don't want to keep you long, but…" His gaze met hers and a soft smile lifted his lips. "I'm hoping you'll say yes to what I'm about to ask."

She twisted her hands in her lap and swallowed.

"If I can get a sitter one night next week, would you go out to dinner with me?" The timidity in his voice was so sweet. Did he actually think she'd say *no*?

"A sitter?"

"My grandparents."

She nodded slightly. "I think we can arrange that."

He blew out a breath and wiped his hands on his jeans. She saw visible relief in his expression. "Great. Is there any place special you'd like to go? Or anything in particular you'd like to eat?"

"I love fish, but it tends to be expensive so I don't buy it as much as I'd like to." She shook her head. "Not that I would order something really expensive."

He reached over and lightly touched the top of her hand. "I'd want you to order whatever you'd like."

Oh, but he was so sweet. He'd genuinely meant every word.

She nodded in appreciation, not trusting her voice.

"Would you rather go to Harry's Stone Grill or Key West Shrimp House? Have you been to either of those places?"

"I've been to Harry's once. It was good." It was with Mom, on Shannon's sixteenth birthday. But she wouldn't think about that now. "Whatever you think."

"Since you've got a hankering for fish, let's visit the Shrimp House this time."

She liked that he'd said *this time*. As though he was already making plans for the two of them to go out again. "That sounds good."

"Is there any day in particular you'd like to go?"

"Not really. Any day would work."

"I'll see if my grandparents can watch them on Thursday, if that's okay with you. I would say Friday, but I'm thinking it might be a little crowded on the weekend."

"Thursday sounds good." Although she hoped she didn't have to wait that long to see him. It would be pure torture. Especially after spending this morning with him, and most of the day tomorrow. She seemed to be developing an addiction to him. He had to be, like, the sweetest guy ever.

"Okay, then." He stood from his chair.

She did likewise.

"I should go now." He said the words, but stared at her instead of leaving.

She knew the feeling. She didn't want him to go either.

"Um, yeah." He glanced down at his hands. He reached up to touch her shoulder, then seemed to think better of it. Did he have in mind to hug her? Kiss her?

She smiled, enjoying what she suspected. "Bye, Wesley."

He nodded. "Goodbye."

She watched as he turned and walked toward his truck. His t-shirt fit him just right, to her thinking, straining slightly against his back and arm muscles. Wow.

No wonder it felt so good when he'd held her on Christopher and Judy's porch swing. It had ended way too soon. She could spend an eternity in those arms. She sighed in contentment.

He stepped up into his truck and waved.

She threw her hand in the air and a smile played on her lips. She was already looking forward to seeing Wesley again tomorrow.

Even if it was at church.

ELEVEN

*B*efore Wesley even had a chance to knock on the door, it flew open. Jaycee stood on the other side, and a grin as wide as the Grand Canyon lit up his face.

Wesley smiled. "Are you ready to go?"

"Yeah, I'm ready. Do we get to ride in your truck?" His eyes zeroed in on Wesley's pickup.

"Sure do."

Jaycee jumped up and pumped his fist in the air.

Oh, to possess the enthusiasm of a five-year-old.

Shannon appeared behind Jaycee, holding Melanie in her arms. "Hi."

Wow. She was gorgeous.

Just her sweet perfume alone was enough to almost knock him off his feet. She smelled good enough to kiss then and there. But he wouldn't. Instead, he drank in the sight before him. Her dress was flattering yet form fitting enough to encourage his mind to go places if he allowed it to. He wouldn't. He refused to think of Shannon as an object. He needed to train his eyes on her lovely face instead.

He could stand there and gaze at her all day. But he should probably greet her. "Hi, beautiful."

Oh, no. He'd said that out loud.

Her gaze dropped and her cheeks blossomed with color.

A sweet smile danced on her lips, but she glanced around him. "Should we…we'll need to put Melanie's car seat in your truck."

"Yeah." He blinked out of his trance. "Of course."

"I can get it!" Jaycee bounced out the door.

"Brighton, go with him and get Jaycee's booster and fasten them in place, please."

Brighton did as asked, leaving the two of them alone. Well, with little Melanie.

"Someone's excited." Wesley smiled.

She rolled her eyes. "You have no idea. He's been bouncing off the walls."

"Did you give him sugar?"

"You'd think so."

He looked over her shoulder. "Do you need anything else out of the house?"

"Just my purse." She turned and retrieved her purse

from the table near the entry, then quickly closed the door. "All ready."

"Okay, let's do this." Excitement surged in his gut.

Shannon's palms perspired as they neared the entrance to the church. She was glad to be holding Melanie in her arms. Especially when she noticed a pretty brunette staring at her Wesley. *Her* Wesley? Where did that come from?

Wesley's warm hand lightly rested on the small of her back as they entered the foyer. Was he letting the brunette girl know they were together?

"Hi, Wesley," the pretty brunette said as she hurried past them. Did she purposely brush against Wesley's arm?

"Hi, Holly." An unreadable expression briefly flashed across his face as he watched her walk off. He guided Shannon and her siblings to a pew near the back. "Just in case you need to take Melanie to the cry room."

She looked to where he pointed, then nodded. "Thank you." Ever the considerate one.

"Is it okay if the boys go to Sunday school? They'll probably enjoy it more than being out here with us."

"Uh, yeah, it's fine with me." She turned to the boys. "Brighton, Jaycee, would you like to go with the other kids?"

Wesley leaned over. "I hear they have popcorn today."

Both boys agreed with a smile.

"I can take them back," Wesley offered.

"Thank you." Shannon sat there awkwardly as Wesley and the boys walked out. She was trying not to notice the brunette and her group of friends staring and whispering about her. Didn't they know they were being rude? She felt like shooting a dirty look in their direction. Instead, she focused on little Melanie. "How long do you think Wesley will be?" She murmured to the little one.

Melanie smiled and Shannon brought her close and kissed her cheek. "You're a good baby."

"Good baby." Melanie threw her arms around Shannon and kissed her cheek in return.

"Oh, you think I'm a good baby too? You little stinker." She tickled Melanie's tummy and she giggled.

Wesley returned and planted himself next to her in the pew. He held out his arms to Melanie and she surprisingly went to him. "I can't believe she's letting me hold her." His voice held pleasure.

"Sometimes she takes a while to warm up to people."

Melanie smacked a kiss on Wesley's cheek. "Good baby."

He chuckled. "I guess that means she likes me?"

Shannon's gaze meandered toward the group of girls still gawking at her and Wesley. She wished they'd just stop. She tried to ignore them and enjoy Wesley's company.

The man standing at the pulpit announced a hymn number and the congregation stood. As the music played, Shannon reached for the hymnal in front of her and turned to the page the song leader had mentioned. She tried to follow along quietly since she didn't exactly know how the tune went. Wesley, on the other hand, seemed to know the song by heart.

She glanced across the room. Apparently, the brunette did too. *Ugh.*

Wesley leaned over and whispered. "I think she might need a change."

She nodded and took Melanie from his arms. Her sister was potty trained for the most part, but Shannon diapered her when they planned to be out for any length of time. Better to be safe than sorry. She pulled a diaper from her purse and took Melanie to the cry room Wesley had pointed out earlier.

Halfway through the diaper change, Holly walked in. "Hi."

Shannon frowned. "Hi." She would have ignored her but she didn't want to be rude.

"I just wanted you to know that Wesley and I…well, we used to have a thing." Why was she telling her this?

Shannon felt like saying, "So?" Instead, she disregarded her comment. No wonder she'd kept staring at Wesley. She clearly wasn't over him yet and she wanted Shannon to know. She should have suspected something when the girl brushed up against him when they'd arrived. *What nerve.*

Shannon gritted her teeth and hurried. She needed to vacate the room as quickly as possible.

"Is she your baby?" Why was this girl so nosy? Was it any of her business? She was likely implying that she was loose. Whatever the case, she was stepping on her last nerve.

She felt like saying, "Mind your own business." But didn't.

"Yes." Shannon instead smiled sweetly. "Mine and Wesley's." She turned and sauntered out of the room, but not before hearing the girl gasp. Shannon smirked. Hopefully, *that* would shut her up. It would either do that or give her and her friends something to *really* gossip about.

She calmly walked back to the pew. A wave of satisfaction surged through her as Wesley slipped his arm around her waist and smiled down at her.

No doubt, they had an audience.

Shannon leaned close and whispered in his ear. "Thank you."

He nodded and took Melanie from her arms. He leaned toward her and briefly glanced toward Holly's group. "It appears we have admirers."

"*You* have admirers," she whispered back.

He moved close and whispered in her ear. "I only want one." His gaze was intent as he spoke and she nearly melted right there on the church pew.

She caught his meaning loud and clear. He held zero interest in Holly. She did her best to ignore the girls for the remainder of the service. It seemed he might just be *her* Wesley after all.

TWELVE

"What did you think of the service?" Mom asked Shannon from across the restaurant lunch table. Wesley was pleased she had gotten along so well with his parents. She was a perfect fit for his family, to his thinking.

"It was interesting." Shannon smiled and shared a smirk with Wesley.

He explained to his mother. "Holly and her friends kept looking over at us." He shook his head. "It was pretty distracting." Although he wanted to say annoying, he didn't want to be rude.

"We tried to ignore them," Shannon said.

"She's jealous, no doubt." Mom looked at him. "Did you tell her?"

He glanced at Shannon. "I think she already suspected. Holly was kind of obvious." He felt he should explain. "We went on a few dates, but I wasn't really interested."

"She certainly seems interested in you."

"Yeah, well, I've got my eye on someone else." He winked at Shannon.

"What did you boys think of Sunday school?" Dad looked to Brighton and Jaycee.

Jaycee was the first to speak. "It was super cool! Shannon, did you know that Jesus walked on the water? Like for reals? I'm not even kidding."

"I've heard that," Shannon said, nodding. "What about you, Brighton? How was your class?"

"I made a new friend. His name is Malachi. I'd never heard that name before," Brighton said.

"It's from the Bible," Wesley told him. "It's actually the last book in the Old Testament."

The waitress came and dropped off the food they'd ordered. After Dad offered a brief prayer, they all dug into their meals. Shannon cut her sandwich into quarters and offered one to Melanie, along with some of her french fries.

"She's a doll," Mom commented.

"I know. She's always been a really good baby." Shannon smiled at Melanie. "It's hard to believe she's my responsibility now. She'll likely grow up thinking I'm her mother."

Mom reached over and touched Shannon's hand. "From what I've seen, you're doing a wonderful job."

"Thank you for saying that. I never imagined I'd be a mother to three at eighteen."

"Shannon, if you need anything—anything—you just let us know, okay?" Mom squeezed her hand then let go.

"Thank you." She blew out a breath and Wesley could tell she was fighting back tears. "That's very kind."

"I mean it," Mom insisted.

Wesley briefly wondered how Shannon's family would be impacted with the Christmas holiday coming up. Grandpa had mentioned something privately about them struggling, and with the comment she'd made at the restaurant, he guessed finances weren't all that great. He couldn't imagine a waitressing salary would be enough to support a family, but what did he know?

Would Shannon be offended if he suggested the gift program at church? He didn't think she'd refuse help, but maybe it would be better to just surprise them. Then again, if she knew the children would get gifts, it might relieve her of a burden. He'd love to lift a burden from her shoulders if he could. Besides, he'd have no idea what kind of gifts to request. If he remembered, he would mention it to her later on when the children weren't within earshot.

"Shannon and I have plans today, so I won't be at

church tonight." Better to inform his parents now so they didn't worry when he didn't show for the service.

Mom and Dad shared a surprised look, and Dad's brow rose, then he nodded. It wasn't like him to skip out on church.

"Wesley said he's going to play basketball with us!" Jaycee grinned.

"Really?" Dad said, looking like he was enjoying the boy's enthusiasm.

"Uh huh, for reals. Even Brighton's happy about it." He looked at his brother. "Huh, Bright?"

Brighton nodded but kept quiet.

Wesley got the feeling Brighton was holding himself back emotionally, and he wondered why. Was he afraid of becoming attached? Wesley could certainly understand that, in light of the loss of their parents.

"Aiden used to play basketball with us," Jaycee volunteered.

Wesley's gaze shot to Shannon. "Aiden?"

"My ex," she explained.

Oh.

"Jaycee." Shannon's tone held a warning. She shook her head and signaled for him to zip his lips.

He'd have to ask her about Aiden later.

Shannon smiled as she prepared the popcorn they'd be enjoying with their movie tonight. She'd never seen a particular movie Wesley had mentioned, so they'd swung by his house and picked up the DVD after lunch.

He'd changed into basketball shorts and an athletic t-shirt, and also grabbed clothes to change into later.

She now glanced out her kitchen window to see Wesley squatting down next to Jaycee, apparently demonstrating how to shoot a free throw.

Having Wesley playing basketball outside with the boys was such a treat for them. It had been months since they'd had a true male role model in their lives, and she felt they desperately needed one. Meeting Wesley had been nothing short of a miracle. Unlike Aiden, Wesley seemed to be thrilled with children.

She looked outside again to see the three high-fiving each other. They appeared to be making their way inside now. Fortunately, the popcorn was ready. Everyone had been too full for supper, after lunch at the restaurant, so they'd all agreed on just a snack. Melanie should be waking up from her nap before too long.

"Mind if I take a shower?" Wesley peeled his shirt away from his chest with his thumb and forefinger. "I'm a little sweaty."

She tried not to notice how attractive he'd looked with it plastered to his skin. But then again, he'd be attractive just about any way.

"A little?" She laughed. "I didn't know you could work up a sweat like that in winter."

"Technically, it's still fall." His voice was teasing.

She shook her head. "Go ahead. The first door on the right once you step into the hallway. There should be towels in the cabinet. And you might want to keep an eye out for spiders."

"Yeah, we have those too. It seems like as soon as the weather turns cold, they run inside."

"I hate that. I don't like to kill them, but if I have the boys relocate them outdoors it seems like they just come right back in. And I certainly don't want them sleeping with me." She shuttered.

"Ah, so you don't like being tickled?" He chuckled.

"No. And definitely *not* by a spider."

He grinned and turned to find the bathroom.

Shannon took the opportunity to quickly tiptoe and peek in on Melanie. The little one rolled around on her bed, talking to her fingers. Shannon just stood there for about ten minutes, watching quietly. Her baby sister was so precious, she hoped she'd be able to raise her right.

A fresh smell and an uncanny feeling like someone was behind her caused Shannon to turn.

"Hi." Wesley smiled. His damp hair was a bit

tousled. Man, he was smoking in his jeans and t-shirt. How did he make such a casual outfit look so good?

"Hi. You take a quick shower." She smiled back, but not before he caught her drinking him in. Her cheeks warmed.

"Momma!" Melanie stood up on her bed and clapped her hands.

Shannon hurried to her before she took a tumble. "No, no. No standing on the bed." She shook her head.

"No, no." Melanie repeated.

"That's right. You could fall down and get hurt. You don't want owies, do you?" Shannon made her sit down, then helped her off the bed.

"Fall down. Get owies." Melanie's eyes grew large as she said the words.

"That's right. So no standing on the bed."

"No standing." Melanie shook her head. "No, no."

"Come here, you little stinker." Shannon scooped her up into her arms and kissed her repeatedly. "You ready to go watch a movie?"

"Watch movie!" She clapped her chubby little hands.

Wesley stretched out his arms to her.

"Do you want to go to Wesley?" Shannon asked.

"No Wesley." Melanie shook her head several times.

He chuckled. "Okay. No Wesley." He puffed out his bottom lip. "Now Wesley is gonna be sad."

"Wesley be sad." Melanie nodded.

Shannon laughed. "She doesn't seem to be feeling your pain."

"Apparently not." He chuckled. "She *is* a little stinker."

Shannon set Melanie down and she ran to her brothers.

"Hey, do you mind if I take the boys out one of these days?" Wesley stuffed his hands in his pockets and attempted to keep the excitement off his face.

"Oh." Surprise lit her countenance. "You'd want to do that? What for?"

He shrugged nonchalantly, as though he didn't have some great scheme in mind. "You know, hang out, do guy stuff."

A gentle smile graced her lips. "That would be wonderful."

"Great. So, Tuesday, after school? Would that work for you?"

"Sure, that sounds awesome." She sucked in a breath. "And Wesley…"

"Yes?"

"Thank you so much. You really don't know how much this means to me. What it will mean to the boys."

"It's my pleasure, Shannon." Anything to bring a smile to her pretty face. She'd had way too much sadness in her life. She deserved a little happiness.

"Ready for the movie? The popcorn is finished. I already dished it into bowls for the kids. I figured we could share the big bowl."

"Sounds good." He surveyed the sectional. "Where should I sit?"

"Next to me?"

"Wouldn't want to be anywhere else." He winked.

Shannon put the movie in and grabbed the remote control. She lowered the lights with a dimmer switch on the wall. The boys had already found their spots and Melanie sat on one side of Shannon after she'd sat down. Wesley staked his claim on the other side.

As soon as the movie started and the boys' attention was riveted on the screen, Wesley draped his arm around the back of the couch. Or around Shannon's shoulders, more accurately. She snuggled into his side, sending his pulse racing. A rush of dopamine must have coursed through him, warming his whole body. If the kids weren't there…

He should focus on the movie, but it was difficult

with Shannon's soft form pressing against him. He really needed a distraction from his thoughts. He reached into the bowl of popcorn and tossed a few kernels into his mouth. The burst of salty sweetness pleased his taste buds.

"This is really good," he whispered in Shannon's ear.

"Thanks. My secret recipe." She turned and grinned up at him.

He stared at her lips. That was a mistake. He couldn't help lowering his lips to hers and indulging in a kiss. His fingers slipped through her hair and his palm held the back of her head, bringing her face closer to his. Her lips were soft and yielding and…

"Are you guys gonna kiss through this whole movie?" The disgusted look on Brighton's face almost made Wesley laugh. He'd change his mind in a few years.

Shannon giggled. "Maybe. Just ignore us and watch the movie, Brighton."

"Are you gonna go to your bedroom again like you did with Aiden?" Jaycee added his two cents.

Wesley wished he hadn't. But he was a five-year-old and five-year-olds tended to speak whatever was on their mind. Wesley wished that hadn't been on Jaycee's mind. Because now it was on *his*.

"Jaycee!" Shannon shot upright. She squeezed her eyes closed and sighed.

Wesley's lips pressed together in a frown. Whoever this Aiden guy was, he *really* didn't like him.

"Just watch the movie, boys, or I'm sending you to bed early." Shannon huffed. She looked at him with an apologetic smile, but she didn't say anything. "No more comments."

But it was too late. Wesley attempted to enjoy the movie after that, as though he hadn't just heard Jaycee's proclamation, but he couldn't. All he could think about was his beautiful Shannon and some guy named Aiden going to her bedroom.

It bothered him. Big time.

Wesley had been silent and kept his distance for the remainder of the movie, no doubt thinking on Jaycee's careless words. Shannon wished she could erase them. She'd read the disappointment in Wesley's eyes, as though the words had crushed his soul.

She worried he might have changed his mind about her. She had to do something, say something to make it right before he left. "Listen, Wesley. About what

Jaycee said. Aiden and I, we dated for a year—"

He held up his hand. "You *really* don't need to explain it to me."

The chill in the night air caused her to shiver. She wished Wesley would pull her close and hold her, like he had when the movie began.

"I-I'm sorry." She felt like weeping.

"Shannon…" His tone was pensive, sad. "Hey, it's fine. Whatever. What's past is past, right? It's not like we can go back and change it."

She frowned. "I just feel like there's this huge wall between us now." She shook her head. "I don't like it."

"Just give me some time to process it, okay?" He blew out a breath. "I need to pray."

"Okay." She stared at the ground. "But…"

He reached over and caressed her cheek all too briefly. "I'll see you on Tuesday, alright?"

"Yeah. Okay." She watched as he climbed into his truck, regret weighing heavy on her soul.

He smiled, but a shadow lingered behind it. He lifted his hand to wave, then drove off.

If only this evening had ended differently.

THIRTEEN

onday morning, Shannon dropped a delighted Melanie off with Judy and Christopher. She'd never seen her little sister take to someone so readily. There was something special about the elderly Amish couple. Well, other than them being Wesley's grandparents.

Thinking of Wesley... She really needed to have a talk with him about her and Aiden's relationship. He needed to know. Everything.

Before she clocked into work, she tried to mentally prepare herself for the day. She'd work till three, pick the boys up at home, then head to Amish country. Judy and Christopher had truly been a Godsend. They'd invited them to stay for dinner tonight. That would be one less meal she would have to cook, and they all enjoyed Christopher and Judy's company.

About an hour into her shift, a familiar face walked through the door.

Aiden.

She sighed, wondering what he wanted. There were other places to eat around town, so why did he keep choosing her place of employment?

He plopped down on one of the seats at the counter. "Hey, Shan. I'll just take a root beer float." He threw the words into the air as she'd walked by.

"One root beer float coming up."

She returned a couple minutes later with his order.

"Sit with me?" His brow shot up.

"Why?" She frowned and returned a stack of menus to their pile.

"I just want to talk."

She shook her head. "I'm working."

His eyes roamed the empty restaurant. "Looks pretty dead to me."

"Maybe, but there are other things I need to do. The ketchup bottles need to be refilled. And the napkins. I have tables to prepare. There are many things that need to be done."

He reached for her hand to stop her. "They can wait, Shan."

She should have noticed when the next customer walked in, but she'd been too distracted. She didn't until he was standing right there. Her eyes widened. "Wesley?"

He stared at her hand, still in Aiden's. And frowned.

She quickly pulled her hand from Aiden's grasp.

"You gonna join me or not?" Aiden asked, briefly glancing at Wesley as if he was of no consequence.

"I already told you no." She stood her ground. "I'm busy."

"Is there a problem, Shannon?" Wesley's brow lowered in clear concern. He placed a hand on her shoulder, studying her face.

She shook her head, then gestured toward Aiden. "Wesley, this is Aiden, my ex. Aiden this is Wesley, my…"

"Her current," Wesley affirmed.

"Current?" Aiden scowled.

"Permanent." Wesley glanced at her and smiled.

She liked the sound of that. Apparently, the prayer had done him good. She didn't catch a hint of the melancholy she'd seen on his face the previous night.

"And I'd appreciate you not trying to make a move on my girl." Wesley stared Aiden down.

My girl?

Aiden held up his hands. "Sheesh. A bit possessive, aren't we?"

Wesley's arms crossed firmly over his chest. He

clearly possessed a physical advantage over Aiden. And right now, he looked like he wanted to show him. "Yeah, I get that way about those I love."

Love? Her heart flip-flopped.

Aiden snorted. "You better watch out for this one, Shan."

Oh, she was watching alright. This was a side of Wesley she'd never seen. And she liked it. Fierce loyalty was a quality she could admire in a man.

Unlike Aiden, who'd bailed at the first hint of responsibility. Wesley, on the other hand, had stepped up to the plate.

"Put this in a to-go cup for me, will you?" Aiden pushed his root beer float toward Shannon. "The customers are a little hostile today."

Wesley cut Aiden a look that conveyed he'd be willing to step outside if need be.

Shannon worried her lip. She'd never had two guys fighting over her. This could go badly.

If Aiden was smart, he'd stop talking.

Shannon set his to-go cup down in front of him, hoping he'd vacate the premises as soon as possible.

"A straw, please?" Aiden's tone caused Wesley to grunt.

She quickly pulled one from her apron pocket and handed it to him.

Aiden stood from the bar stool. "I'd leave you a tip but—"

"You'll leave her a tip anyway," Wesley demanded, working his jaw.

"Wesley," she whispered the desperate plea, shaking her head.

"You have nerve. You know I could have you thrown out of this restaurant," Aiden threatened Wesley. He looked at Shannon. "Who does he think he is?"

"Aiden, just go. Please." Shannon couldn't lose this job. And with the way Aiden and Wesley were behaving, that could be a very real possibility.

He pulled a five-dollar bill out of his pocket and grudgingly plopped it on the counter. "Keep the change."

Shannon sighed in relief when Aiden finally exited the restaurant.

Wesley's brow furrowed and he thumbed over his shoulder. "So, *that* was Aiden?"

"Yes. And we need to talk. I want to clear the air after what happened last night."

"Okay."

"Do you need to be somewhere soon? I'm not really due for a break for a couple of hours."

"I can sit at a booth and bring my laptop in. That's the beauty of my job. It goes with me and I can do it anywhere."

"Great. Would you like coffee?"

He stepped near and lightly caressed her cheek with his thumb, sending shivers down her spine. "Yes, please. I'll hold off on breakfast, though, until you take your break."

She nodded. "I'll bring your coffee out to you."

Wesley sat in a corner booth, half working and half admiring Shannon's interaction with her customers. She really was an amazing young woman. He found himself wanting to know everything about her.

"Here you go. Does it look right?" She smiled, placing his breakfast platter on the table.

His eyes slowly roamed her face, then he took the rest of her in. "It looks perfect."

"You didn't even look at the plate." Her hand situated on her hip.

"Don't need to."

She shook her head, a smile playing on her lips, then slid in the booth across from him.

"You're sharing this with me," he insisted. "That's why I got the big breakfast platter."

He bowed his head and prayed aloud for the food,

but silently he asked forgiveness for his jealousy and short temper with Aiden earlier.

"Thank you." Shannon took a bite of the English muffin.

"My pleasure." He nodded slightly. "Go ahead. Tell me whatever's on your mind." He dug into his eggs, but trained his eyes on her.

"Well, okay. Aiden and I dated for about a year or so. Before Mom and Dad, well…" He gathered she was trying to get through this without crying. "Anyway, he sounded like he wanted to get serious and all that. I thought maybe he might propose. He came over after, you know…"

He nodded. "Your parents."

She swallowed. "Yeah. And I was pretty torn up. He was comforting at first."

"At first?"

"Yeah. Apparently, we weren't on the same page. What he meant by going to the next level was not the same as what I thought."

"Which brings us to your bedroom." He could hurt the guy.

"Well, yeah. He wanted to, but I said no. After that, he was different. He said he was too young to take on the responsibility of an instant family. He even suggested putting the kids in foster care. Can you even imagine? I would never abandon them, especially after we'd just lost Mom and Dad. They would have been devastated." She shuttered and brushed away a tear.

He reached across the table and took her hand. "You did the right thing."

"I know. But it's been really hard." Twin tears raced down her cheeks now. "I can hardly put food on our table. And the bills just seem to keep coming. DCS has come by a couple of times. I'm just afraid that if I get sick or something…What would happen? I don't want them to take my siblings away."

"That's not going to happen."

"You don't know that."

"Didn't your parents have a life insurance policy or anything?"

She nodded. "My dad did, but it wasn't much. I paid for the funerals and then I was advised to pay some toward the house and for future insurance payments. It certainly helped because it lowered the house payment. I wouldn't have been able to afford what Dad had been paying."

"How about other family? Or didn't your parents have friends that could have helped you?"

She shrugged. "My mom has a sister over on the west coast. She offered to move us over there." She shook her head. "I didn't want to leave the only home we've ever known and go someplace foreign. It would have been too big of an adjustment for the kids."

"I understand."

"She did send us some money. I bought the boys' school clothes and supplies with that and filled up my tank with gas a few times. Their friends brought food by for a few days after the funeral. But that only lasts so long."

"I see." His mind volleyed for words of encouragement. "You know I will help you out any way I can. You don't have to do this alone."

"Wesley…" She shook her head. "I can't ask you to—"

"You didn't ask. And I insist. Don't think you're going to change my mind."

"You're stubborn, you know that?" She laughed.

"One of my best qualities." He raised his eyebrows twice.

She aimed a fork in his direction. "What am I going to do with you?"

"Well, to start, I'm hoping to get a kiss. Before I leave? Please?"

"Hmm…" She tapped her chin. "I'll have to think about that one."

"You do that. I like it when I'm on your mind." He winked. "But do it while you're eating, because I don't want you to go hungry."

Shannon returned to work fifteen minutes later, but not before delighting him with the kiss he'd been hoping for all morning. Their conversation had solidified his determination to take care of her and her siblings, and it confirmed to him that it was, indeed, God who had brought them together.

God, is Shannon the one?

It sure seemed like things were leaning in that direction, although he'd never be able to fully commit unless she became a Christian. He needed to pray. Urgently.

FOURTEEN

"Wesley," Dad's voice echoed from the living room.

Wesley poked his head out of his bedroom. "Yeah, Dad?"

"Come here. Your mother and I would like to talk to you."

"Sure." He stepped out into the hallway and made his way to where Mom and Dad sat. Looking rather serious. What was going on?

He planted himself on the couch when he realized this was going to be more than just a quick chat.

"How well do you know Shannon?" Dad stared at him intently, and Wesley attempted to read his expression. Was he disappointed about something?

He shrugged. "Pretty well, I think."

"Pretty well?" Mom's tone held doubt. Or was it an accusation?

He looked from Mom to Dad. Why on earth were they acting so strangely? Where were they going with this conversation? "What is this about?"

"You haven't slept with her?" Dad's gaze was piercing.

"Slept…? What?" His hand plowed through his hair. How fast did they think he moved? And why would they even ask him such a thing? They'd known him all his life. "No!"

"There are rumors going around." Mom frowned.

"Rumors? About *me*?"

"You and Shannon." Dad nodded. "Everyone thinks Melanie is your baby. That you're living in sin."

Heat warmed his face. "*What*?"

"Are you not telling us something, son?" Dad stared at him. "You can talk to us about anything, you know."

"Dad, I haven't slept with *anybody*. Ever." He shook his head. "Whoever is making up these rumors is lying."

"It's Shannon." Mom stated, staring a hole right through his heart.

"Shannon?" His heart sunk to his stomach.

Mom nodded. "She apparently told Holly that Melanie was your child. And hers."

Had the two of them even spoken?

"Why would she do that?" It was unbelievable, really.

"I don't know. Attention, maybe?" Mom shook her head. "All I know is that you probably need to set things straight if you want to salvage your reputation. And maybe you need to think twice about your relationship with Shannon."

"Now you know why the girls were staring during church," Dad commented.

Wesley's head spun. He'd worked *so* hard to stay pure, to be a good example. All his involvement with the youth…trying to encourage them to keep themselves from the devil's snares…all of that would be undermined now. Called into question. They'd surely think him a hypocrite of the worst kind.

Why would Shannon do this?

He shook his head and pressed his lips together. He needed to have a talk with her. The sooner the better.

Wesley forced himself to exercise restraint by not pounding on the door. So many thoughts and emotions had whirled through his head since his parents had shared the news with him. He barely gotten a wink of sleep. He'd *thought* God had brought him and Shannon together, but now he was questioning everything. He had to remain calm so they could have a rational conversation. But he didn't feel rational at the moment. No, he was disappointed. Upset. Desperate.

The door finally opened to him.

Shannon's expression told him she'd read his mind without him saying a word. "Wesley? Is something wrong? Is everything okay?" Her tone was worrisome.

"No, everything is not okay." He wouldn't raise his voice. He. Would. Not. "You told Holly that Melanie was my baby?"

"Yes, I did." She'd spoken the words like there was nothing wrong with them. Like it was perfectly okay to go around telling people things that weren't true.

His temperature must have risen a few degrees, because he was suddenly very hot. "Why? Why would you make up a lie?"

"I wanted to shut her up. She was pis—" Her lips smashed together. "She was making me upset."

"So you told her we *slept* together?" His voice practically screeched.

"No. Well…" She sighed and shook her head. "I didn't mean for it to sound like that."

"How did you mean for it to sound?" He'd determined not to raise his voice, but it was *really* difficult. More difficult by the second, in fact.

"Wesley, she followed me into the cry room. Then

she asked me if Melanie was my baby. Like she just assumed I was *that* kind of girl. So I told her yes, Melanie belonged to you and me."

"I don't understand why you would say that." His heartbeat showed no sign of slowing down.

"She was annoying me, and it was none of her business."

"Asking if Melanie is your baby is a perfectly legitimate question."

"Now you're taking *her* side? She practically accused me of sleeping around!"

"Is that what she said?"

"No, but it was implied."

"And so you…" He huffed and shook his head so hard he thought he just might give himself a headache. "I can't believe this!"

"Why is this such a big deal to you? Is the thought of the two of us having a baby together so terrible?"

"Shannon…" She had *no* idea how hard he fought against his fleshly desires. The other night on the couch…

He sighed. "I don't know what I'm going to do now."

"About *what*?" She still didn't get it.

"Don't you see? My reputation's been ruined."

"What?"

"I look like a hypocrite. Here, I've been teaching the youth to abstain from immorality. And now… Shannon, why would you do this?"

"You act like I've attacked you personally. I didn't mean for this to be a big deal. At all. I had no idea your reputation would suffer. I thought you'd find it funny, actually."

"Funny?" He squeezed his eyes shut. "No, there is nothing humorous about this. *A good name is rather to be chosen than great riches.*"

"What do you want me to do? I can tell Holly it was just a joke, if that makes you feel better."

"I don't know if there's anything you can do. The damage has already been done. Even if we tell people the truth now, not everyone is going to believe it. There will still be that seed of doubt in people's minds."

She lifted her hands. "I don't know how to make this right, Wesley."

"To tell the truth, I'm disappointed in you." There, he'd said it.

"Wesley, if you're looking for the perfect girl, I can assure you that I am not her."

"I'm not asking for perfection." Was he?

"Really? Because it sounds to me like that's *exactly* what you're looking for." Tears shimmered in her eyes and her chin quivered. "If you're going to dump me, please, just do it now. These kids don't need another heartbreak."

And just like that, his resolve crumbled.

Is that what she thought? That he was dumping her? He needed to make things right.

He gentled his tone and approached her. "The kids don't, or *you* don't?"

"Both."

"Hey, now." He stepped close and touched her shoulder, then reached out and brushed her tears with the pads of his thumbs. "I'm not dumping you. You'll have to do a lot worse than that to get rid of me."

He opened his arms now and pulled her to his chest.

"I'm sorry." She sobbed.

He felt like a jerk. "No, I'm the one who should be sorry. Forgive me for overreacting?"

She nodded. "If you'll forgive me for saying what I did."

"Already have."

He lifted her chin, and stared into her glistening eyes. "I'm going to kiss you now."

She nodded and smiled through her tears. "I'm probably going to kiss you back."

"Okay." He grinned and lowered his lips to hers.

FIFTEEN

Christopher eyed his wife over the bowl of delicious beef stew she'd prepared. Nothing like a hot bowl of stew on a cold day to warm up his insides. "Judy, how did your time with the *boppli* go today?"

Her face lit up like an *Englischer's* Christmas lights. "*Wunderbaar*! That little one is just a sweet doll."

"I'm worried that you might be getting too attached."

"*Ach*, do not worry about me, husband. That family needs us."

"I think maybe we might need them just as much, *ain't so*?" His throat burned, but it wasn't because of the stew. That happened every now and then when he thought about the past and all the mistakes he'd made.

"She remind you of her too?"

"Little Katie?" He nodded. "Very much so."

"And Jaycee is so much like our Kendal."

"Could be his brother. But his brother…" He let his voice trail off. Kendal's brother, Wesley's *dat*, had been the only one of the *kinner* to survive the accident that fateful day. Then he rejected the church to live in the world. Out of the three they'd lost, his departure had been the worst.

"You miss him, ain't so?"

"I miss them all. Especially this time of year. We have so many *gut* memories. Remember when Kendal had the part in the school's Christmas program?"

"*Jah*, he stole the show."

"I don't think his teacher expected him to jump onto the audience like that. Neither did the audience." He chuckled. "That *bu* was something else."

"Well, we did tell him that, with *Gott*, all things were possible. He really did believe he could fly. Can't fault a boy for having too much faith."

"No. Some have too much. Others have too little."

Judy instinctively understood the shift in conversation. She could practically read his mind. "You know that he goes to a church. Has for a long time."

He shook his head. "But it is not a Plain church."

"Don't you think it's time? Life is too short, Christopher." Tears pricked her eyes. "Our son is alive, yet we treat him like he is dead."

"What do you want me to do? You know my hands are tied."

"But you are the bishop. If the other leaders will listen to anyone's suggestion, it would be yours."

"I don't think I can change their minds. The shunning is what Jacob Ammon stood for. It is what sets us apart. You know that's the way we have always done it."

"What if the way we've always done it is wrong? What about what Jesus stood for? What about *love*?"

"If you think I do not love my son, you are *ab im kopp, fraa*."

"Then do something about it. Show him. I assure you that what he has been receiving from us is not love." His *fraa's* reprimand stung. But she spoke truth. "Has it not been a joy getting to know Wesley these last few years? He is just like his father."

"I know."

"Maybe *Der Herr* brought this little family into our lives for a greater purpose. Maybe it's not just about helping them, but about opening our eyes to all we've lost."

"*Ach*, you make too much sense."

"That's why you married me, *schatzi*." She teased now.

"I will pray about it. Only by a miracle will the *Bann* be lifted."

"Last I heard, *Der Herr* was still in the business of miracles. And this is the Season for miracles, ain't so? I will pray with you."

Christopher didn't miss the hopefulness behind his *fraa's* smile. *Jah*, he'd pray with everything in him. It would take a miracle indeed.

SIXTEEN

If Wesley wasn't careful, he could see himself addicted to spending time with Shannon and her siblings. Being with them seemed so natural. "Before I leave, I'd like to have a talk with you."

"Didn't we already?"

"A different kind of talk." He glanced at the children in the other room. "But not until after the kids go to bed."

"Well, they need to go to bed soon anyway." She clapped her hands and they walked into the living room, commanding the boys' attention. "Alright, time for bed now."

"Aww…" Jaycee protested. "Already?"

"Yes. And no arguing. Wesley and I need to talk."

Brighton snorted. "I think she means kiss."

"Brighton." It was the warning tone again. Shannon cast an apologetic look at Wesley.

Wesley raised his eyebrows and smiled. "Hey. That sounds good to me."

Shannon shook her head and tossed a couch pillow at him. "Don't encourage him." She turned to Brighton. "We *are* planning to talk. Now off to bed."

"Are you going to read to us tonight?" Jaycee complained.

"No, not tonight. Now scoot. And don't forget to brush your teeth."

"And say your prayers," Wesley added for good measure.

"But we don't usually say prayers." Brighton stared at Wesley.

"Why not start now?" Wesley suggested.

"How?"

"I'll show you, if you'd like."

"Uh…" Brighton's gaze flitted from Wesley to Shannon, then back. He shrugged. "Okay, I guess."

"I want to pray too!" Jaycee puffed out his chest as if he was in on some top-secret mission.

"Okay, point me to your bedrooms." Wesley smiled.

"We only have one. The boys have to share," Brighton said glumly.

Wesley nodded. "My brother and I shared when we were younger too."

"You have a brother?" Brighton's head tilted sideways.

"Sure do. He's off at college right now, so now I get the room all to myself."

Jaycee sighed dramatically. "It'll be a lo-o-o-ng time before Brighton goes off to college. I'll never get my own room."

"It'll be here before you know it, buddy. Trust me." Wesley followed the boys down the hall. "Hey, this is a pretty cool bedroom. Do those stars glow in the dark?" He pointed to the ceiling.

"Yeah, they're super cool! Sometimes I pretend like I'm in a spaceship flying through the galaxy." The excitement in Jaycee's voice was palpable.

"Well, I think it's perfect for praying," Wesley said.

"How come?"

"Well, because God lives in Heaven and that's way up in the sky, and God made all the stars. Do you know how many stars there are?"

Jaycee scratched his head. "Um, two thousand?"

"More like a billion, Jaycee," Brighton interjected.

"Actually, counting the stars that scientists actually know about, they say there is at least enough for each person on earth to own eleven trillion."

"Whoa! I can't even count that high." Jaycee laughed.

Wesley smiled. "I can't either. It's a lot. And Heaven is past all those stars. But even though it's far away, God can see us right here, right now."

"How?" Brighton asked.

"Well, because He's God. He doesn't have limitations like we do. He can be everywhere at the same time."

"Whoa," Jaycee exclaimed.

"We should probably pray now before your sister loses patience with us and kicks me out." He chuckled.

"She won't kick you out, she likes you too much. She talks about you *all* the time. Are you gonna get married?"

Wesley chuckled at Jaycee's plethora of comments. "Whoa. Where did that question come from? You know what, never mind. We'd better pray now."

"What do we do?"

"First of all, let's turn off the light so we can see those awesome stars." Wesley nodded for Brighton to hit the switch. "Now, come and kneel next to the bed."

"How come?" Wesley didn't mind all Jaycee's questions one bit. In fact, he welcomed them.

"Because if you lie down to pray, you'll probably fall asleep like I do." He knelt and folded his hands to show the boys. He could barely see them in the dark. He'd keep it short, although if he was praying alone, he'd say much more. "Now, you just talk to God like this, but you can say whatever is on *your* mind. *'Dear*

God, We come before You to give You praise. Thank You for who You are and for everything You've given me, especially for my home in Heaven. Thank You for letting me meet my super cool new friends, Brighton and Jaycee. And their sisters too. Thank You for the food you gave me to eat today and for watching over me. In Jesus name, Amen.' It can be as long or as short as you want it to be. Just tell God whatever is on your heart."

"Okay. I want to pray now. But, do you mind if I pray in private?" Jaycee asked.

"Yeah, me too," Brighton said.

"Nope, not at all. God can hear you even if you don't say the words out loud." Wesley nodded.

"You can go kiss my sister now." Brighton's sly look nearly made Wesley laugh.

"Thank you for your permission. But I think I need her permission too." He chuckled. "Goodnight, boys. Sleep well."

"Goodnight, Wesley. Come back tomorrow, okay?" Jaycee said. Both boys looked at him expectantly.

"We'll see." He stepped out of the room and closed the door behind him.

"There you are," Shannon whispered. "Melanie's already asleep."

"The boys are praying. They should go down soon."

"Thank you for doing that with them. They really look up to you. Not just Jaycee, but Brighton too."

"Yeah, I kinda got that feeling. I hope I don't disappoint them."

"You won't. From what I know of you, you are a good man, Wesley."

"Whoa. Don't go putting me up on a pedestal. I am just a sinner saved by grace. If it weren't for Jesus, I'd be a mess. Whatever good you see in me, that's Christ."

"I'm not sure I understand all that religious stuff. But you don't need to explain it to me."

"Okay." He held up his hands. "No pressure from me."

"So, what was it that you wanted to talk about?"

Wesley followed Shannon into the living room and they both took a seat on the sectional. "How do you feel about being part of the Christmas project?"

"Christmas project? What's that?"

"It's something that all the community churches participate in. People in need sign up and people in the churches try to provide for those needs. It's mainly just buying Christmas gifts for the children."

"They buy Christmas gifts for *other* people's children?" Her eyes widened.

"Yes. Probably not anything super expensive like a laptop or anything. But they do ask what the children would like. Are you interested?"

"I don't know." She frowned. "I just...I feel like such a charity case already with everything that you and your grandparents have done for us."

"There's nothing wrong with charity, especially when you really need it. Besides, this is for the kids."

"But I feel bad taking when I have nothing to give back," she lamented.

"You're looking at it all wrong."

"What do you mean?" She leaned back and clutched a throw pillow to her chest.

"Do you know the meaning of the word charity?"

She shrugged and guessed. "To give to those less fortunate?"

"Well, yeah that's one definition. But I was talking about the Biblical definition."

"No, I don't know that one."

"It means *a love that costs something* or *love in action*. In essence, an act of true love. Most people consider it a blessing to give to those in need."

"I don't know, Wesley..." She sighed.

"They *want* to help you out, Shannon. We believe it is more blessed to give than to receive. Truly. That's how Christians show the love of Jesus. And what better time to show His love than when we celebrate His birth? Jesus' entire life and legacy was about giving.

135

That's why He came to earth."

She frowned. "I'm not sure I understand all that. I don't really even know that much about Jesus."

"Do you want to?" Because if she didn't want to know, he wouldn't push. But if she did… *God, please speak to Shannon's heart.*

"Yeah, sure. I guess."

"Okay, well, what do you already know about Jesus?"

"Well, He's supposed to be the baby in the manger, right? And He's supposed to be the one who is on the crosses, like on jewelry and paintings." She shook her head. "I probably sound like a complete idiot."

"No, not at all. Yes, Jesus was born in a manger, and He was the one on the cross." He smiled. "But do you know *why* He came?"

"To save us from our sins?"

"That's right. He was literally born to die. To offer Himself as a sacrifice for our sins." He nodded. "But the story actually started at the beginning of the world."

"It did?"

"Well, God has always been, but the human story began then. In the very beginning of life on earth, God created Adam and Eve and put them in The Garden of Eden. He gave them a choice. They chose to disobey God and were kicked out of the garden. Until then,

Adam had perfect fellowship with God. But at the point that Adam sinned, he brought sin upon the entire human race. So, everyone who has been born after that, beginning with Adam and Eve's children, is born with a sin nature. We are all sinners.

"Cain was the first person born. He was also the first murderer. He killed his brother, Abel, because he was jealous of him. See, they both brought a sacrifice to God. God accepted Abel's sacrifice because he brought what God required – blood. Cain brought vegetables and God rejected Cain's sacrifice."

"Vegetables?"

"Well, he brought produce, whatever he'd grown in the garden."

"Why did God reject Cain's but not Abel's?"

"Because a blood sacrifice is required to atone for sin. *Without the shedding of blood, there is no remission,* the Bible says. It has to be blood."

"Why?"

"I'm guessing it comes back to the word charity. A love that costs you something, a costly love. I think it was probably a lot more painful to have to kill an innocent animal than to pull up a basket of veggies. And I believe that back then, animals and mankind had a much closer relationship than we do now. Animals were not afraid of humans and vice versa. It was also a picture of us trying to reach God by going about it our own way. We can't reject what God has told us to do and then expect Him to reward us. We, like Cain, must do what is required." He shrugged. "But even then God gave Cain the chance to make things right, to bring the sacrifice He required."

"But he didn't?"

"No. He got angry and killed his brother. He placed a curse on himself."

"So, when we sin, we curse ourselves?"

"Wow, that's good insight. But yes, you're totally right." He nodded.

"But *you* don't offer sacrifices or anything, do you?" Her lips twisted.

He wouldn't laugh at her expression. Her questions were precious, though.

"No. Jesus was my sacrifice. *That's* why He died on the cross."

"What?" Her head tilted to one side.

"Up until the time when Jesus came, men were still required to offer animal sacrifices. It was something that they had to do every year. If you read the story of Jesus' birth, Joseph and Mary brought a sacrifice to the temple."

"Really?"

He nodded. "But Jesus' death fulfilled the righteous

demands of the law. When He died, He offered Himself as a sacrifice, once and for all. For all men, for all time. Understand?"

"Kind of?"

He chuckled. "You don't sound too confident."

She shook her head.

"The sacrifice God required was one without spot or blemish, so for Jesus to fulfill that requirement, He had to be perfect, sinless. Which He was. The Bible says He was tempted in all points, yet He was without sin."

"Wow."

"I know, right? I sin every day. Like automatically."

"You do?"

He laughed now. "You have no idea. And that's exactly why I needed Jesus to save me. I could never get into Heaven on my own, because I'm a sinner. But when I accepted Jesus' offer to pay for those sins, He took them upon Himself. Now, when I stand before God when this life is over, He will accept me because of what Christ did."

"How do you know that?"

"Because God says so in His Word, the Bible."

"Oh." She frowned. "Well, what about me and everyone else who doesn't go to church and read the Bible and all that? Do I...does that mean that I won't go to Heaven?"

"Well, I think you're getting works mixed up with salvation. Those are two totally different things."

"They are?"

"Yes. Salvation, or to be saved, meaning you are going to Heaven, has only one requirement."

"What is it?"

"Believe on the Lord Jesus Christ, and thou shalt be saved. Basically, you trust Jesus to save you. He pays for your sins, so you don't have to."

"But I already believe in Jesus. I've never doubted that He's real or anything. And I believe in God. I'm not an atheist. So, I guess I don't really understand."

"Well, intellectual faith is not enough. The Bible says that even the devils believe, and tremble. A faith that saves is one that you believe with your whole heart. And when that happens, you are born again."

"I've heard that term before but I don't quite understand it."

"Remember I told you we inherit Adam's sin nature?"

She nodded.

"The Bible says we are dead in trespasses and sins. It is a spiritual death, a separation from God. The spirit is what becomes born again when you trust Jesus to save you. Your spirit is revived because God's Spirit comes to live inside you and that fellowship with God is restored."

"God's Spirit?"

"Yes. And you will *know* when God's Spirit is living inside you."

"How?"

"Well, I got saved when I was about seventeen. I used to party, go watch bad movies, drink alcohol, all kinds of things. But when Jesus came to live inside me, I no longer found pleasure in those things. I want to do what He wants me to do now. All that stuff I used to do didn't bring glory to God. As a child of God, I have a chance to earn rewards in Heaven."

"Rewards in Heaven? Okay, that just went way over my head."

"I'm talking too much. I'm sorry, but talking about what Jesus has done for me excites me."

She laughed. "I can tell."

"But it all boils down to this. Everyone needs to be saved. If we're not, we have no hope of Heaven."

"And if we don't go to Heaven?"

"There is only one other place to go." He frowned.

"Hell?"

"Well, actually hell is a temporary place. The final destination for those who reject Christ is the Lake of Fire."

Her eyes grew large. "A lake of fire? That sounds scary."

"It is. And it's not something anyone should mess around with. If God says something in His Word is true and real, you better believe that it is. God cannot lie."

"Wow. I definitely don't want to go there."

"Me neither."

"Why does God make people go there? It sounds so horrible."

"God doesn't *make* anyone go there. God is not willing that anyone should perish. That's why He sent Jesus. Everyone who is in Hell has made a conscious *choice* to reject God's free gift of salvation. It's free! It doesn't even make any sense to me that people would reject it when it's totally *free* for them. Christ has already suffered so they don't have to. Jesus paid it all. Hell and the Lake of Fire were intended for the devil and his angels."

"So, that's where the devil is?"

"Not yet, but he will be."

She shuttered. "I don't even like to think about that."

"Me neither. But I sure do love thinking about how wonderful Heaven is going to be!"

"Wesley, I want to go to Heaven too." Her eyes shimmered with moisture.

He released a heavy sigh, relief flooding him. "Thank you! I could kiss you right now. But I won't. Yet." He felt like shouting, "Glory, Hallelujah!"

She smiled.

"If you want to go to Heaven, it's as simple as trusting Jesus. Confess with your mouth, believe in your heart."

"Will you pray with me?"

"I'd love to." He reached for her hands and they both bowed their heads.

SEVENTEEN

Wesley couldn't wipe the grin off his face as he drove toward Shannon's house. He knew that he and the boys would have a good time today, and he couldn't wait to see the look on Shannon's face when they returned home from their excursion. He'd made sure to bring along his camera so he could share the special moments with her at a later time.

As soon as he drove up, Jaycee and Brighton shot out of the house. Shannon tagged behind them with Melanie in her arms. She walked up to the driver's side window as the boys piled in the truck.

"I think if they had to wait another minute, they would burst," Shannon said. He loved her smile.

"I might be just as excited as they are." Wesley grinned in return.

"Jaycee, grab your booster out of the car first."

"Ah, I hate that thing. I want to ride in the truck like a big person."

She held up her hands and shrugged. "Sorry."

"It's the law," Wesley added. "You don't want me to get a ticket, do you?"

"No, I guess not," Jaycee grumbled, but retrieved his seat anyway.

"It'll be worth it. I promise." Wesley said the words to Jaycee, but he winked at Shannon.

"Just what do you have planned for today?" Shannon's lips twisted.

"Nope. That's top-secret information." Wesley teased. "You'll find out soon enough."

"Well, you three have fun, then." Shannon waved to the boys.

He wasn't about to leave without giving her a kiss. He leaned out the window and briefly kissed her lips. "I'll miss you."

The boys waved goodbye to their sister as Wesley backed up out of the driveway.

Brighton turned to Wesley once they were on the road. "What *are* we doing?"

"First, we're going to go find something special for your sister for Christmas. I need you two to help me pick something out. Then after that, I figured we'd go get some pizza."

"Pizza!" Both boys whooped and hollered.

Apparently, that had been a good choice for their meal. He planned to let them play some of the games at the kids' pizza place too, but he'd keep that part a surprise.

"And then I have another surprise. But we can't go there until last."

"For reals?" Jaycee bounced. "Where? Where?"

Wesley shook his head. "Not telling. You're gonna have to wait."

He clapped his hands together. "This is gonna be the best day ever! Huh, Brighton?"

Brighton shrugged. "I guess."

"This is fun! Thank you for bringing us here. And for getting something special for my sister." Brighton slipped a token into a game of skeet ball, between Jaycee and Wesley.

"Yeah, it's super cool! Thank you, Wesley! I think you might be my favorite. Well, after Santa," Jaycee exclaimed.

Wesley chuckled and tossed a ball into the five-thousand-point hole. "You're welcome. I'm glad you're having a good time. Now remember, Jaycee, you can't tell Shannon that we got her something. It needs to be a surprise, okay?"

"Okay."

"No hints, either," Brighton warned.

"I won't tell. For reals," Jaycee asserted.

"Well, we need to scoot if we're going to go to our last destination. Are you guys ready to turn your tickets in and claim your prizes?"

"I still have a couple of tokens," Brighton said.

"Me too," said Jaycee.

"Do you want to give them to the little girl over there?" Wesley suggested, nodding to a young girl standing and watching someone else play one of the games. "I don't think she got to play very much."

"Okay."

They walked to the little girl and handed her the tokens. Her face illuminated like one of the arcade games. "Thank you!"

Jaycee beamed as they walked to the prize counter. "She was really happy."

Wesley slid a glance at both boys. "Doesn't it feel good to make someone happy?"

"Yeah, it does," Brighton said.

Jaycee nodded. "I like to make people happy, just like Santa!"

Wesley didn't correct him. Someday he might, when the time was right, and with Shannon's permission. It was difficult to fathom that the Parker family grew up being told about Santa Claus, yet they had no clue about the true meaning of the season. The thought brought sadness to his heart. How many more children out there had never heard about God's love gift to the world? He'd just taken for granted growing up in a Christian home.

He needed to think of a way to show these boys what Christmas was all about. He could read them the Christmas story, but he wanted it to be memorable for them, he wanted it to be real. Just then, an idea popped into his mind. Excitement bubbled in his chest at the thought of making his idea a reality.

As soon as the boys redeemed their tickets for prizes, they headed for the truck.

"Are you two ready for our last stop?" He maneuvered out of the parking lot and onto the main road.

"Yeah, yeah! Where is it? Where is it?"

Wesley laughed at Jaycee's enthusiasm. "It's a ways away. It might be a while before we get there. And it's gonna take some big muscles."

"Brighton has big muscles. Show him, Brighton," Jaycee boasted, nudging his brother.

"They're not big compared to Wesley's, Jaycee."

"Let me see," Wesley encouraged. "Flex for me."

Brighton and Jaycee both rolled up their sleeves and did as told.

Wesley grinned. "Hey, that's pretty good! Must be all that basketball playing."

"Brighton's real strong," Jaycee asserted.

"I don't think *my* muscles were that big when I was your age," Wesley said.

"For reals?" Jaycee looked at Brighton, his eyes sparkling. "You're going to have bigger muscles than Wesley!"

Wesley nodded. "Probably. And you're going to need those muscles to cut down and carry the tree we're going to get."

"We're going to get a tree?" There was no end to Jaycee's excitement.

"We get to cut it down too?" Brighton eyed Wesley.

"That's right." Wesley nodded.

"But Shan said we don't have money for a tree." Jaycee frowned.

"It's my gift to you," Wesley insisted.

"But you already got us pizza and let us play lots of games."

He chuckled. "Just don't expect it all the time or I'll go broke."

Shannon peeked out the window when lights from a vehicle flashed on the wall. Wesley and the boys were back! She couldn't wait to hear about the adventures they'd had. She imagined Jaycee's excitement and smiled just thinking about it.

Wesley sure had been a blessing in their lives. He'd told Aiden he was permanent. She just hoped he'd never change his mind. Because being with somebody like Wesley would be a dream come true.

"Shan! Shan!" Jaycee burst through the door with a smile larger than life. "You'll never guess what we got! And Brighton and I did it all by ourselves!"

She laughed and met Wesley's gaze as he walked in with Brighton. "Did what?"

"Come to the truck. You'll see," Wesley beckoned. He turned to Brighton and Jaycee. "Do you think we should make her wear a blindfold?"

"Yeah!" Jaycee jumped.

"How about if I just close my eyes and you can lead me by the hand?" she suggested.

Wesley glanced over her shoulder into the house. "Where's Melanie?"

"She's asleep already. I didn't expect you three to be out this late. It *is* a school night." She looked at the boys.

"Ah…does that mean we'll have to wait?" Jaycee whined.

"Wait for what?"

Wesley put his finger to his lips, aiming a *shh* at Jaycee.

"I think you just need to come with us right now. You'll see." Wesley reached for her hand. "Now, close your eyes."

Wesley pulled her along until, she guessed, they were standing near his truck. He let go of her hand and it sounded like he was opening the tailgate. *Oh.*

"Okay, open your eyes."

"I can smell it." She said, her eyes still closed. "It's a Christmas tree!" She opened them to find her assumption correct.

Jaycee nodded. "Uh huh, and Brighton and me cut it down and carried it all the way back to the truck!"

"Brighton and I," she corrected. "It sounds like you three had a lot of fun."

"We had the best time ever!" Jaycee was such a ball of energy, Shannon wondered how on earth she'd get him to calm down enough to go to sleep.

"Did you boys tell Wesley thank you?"

Jaycee practically plowed Wesley over, throwing his hands around his waist. "Thank you, Wesley!"

Brighton's hug was much more subdued, but he offered his thanks as well.

"It was my pleasure." He looked at Shannon and

grinned. "I think I had just as good a time as the boys had."

"Can we decorate it right now?" Jaycee bounced.

"We need to get it into some water." Wesley turned to Shannon. "Do you have a tree stand?"

"Yes, but it's in the attic."

"I can get it," Brighton volunteered.

"It's already past your bedtime. We can get it out of the attic tomorrow."

"Sure." Wesley nodded. "Do you have a large bucket then?"

She nodded. "We can use the one we have for washing cars. Brighton, will you grab it from the garage?"

"Okay." They watched as Brighton hurried to the garage with Jaycee close behind him.

Wesley reached for her hand. "I'm sorry I kept them out so late."

"Oh no, it's fine. It's not every day they get to hang out with a cool older brother."

He chuckled. "Cool older brother, huh? I think I like the sound of that."

Shannon's cheeks warmed when she realized what her comment implied, although that wasn't how she'd meant it. Because, if she and Wesley did have a future together, he would indeed become the boys' brother-in-law.

"I didn't mean…" She let her words fall off.

"I hoped you did." His fingers lightly brushed her cheek. "I meant it when I said permanent. And after what happened last night, I'm even more sure of it."

"You are?" She swallowed.

"One hundred percent." He leaned close and briefly brushed her cheek with his lips. "Should we get this thing in some water now?" He pulled the tree from the truck bed.

She nodded. "Will you come help us decorate it tomorrow night?"

He grimaced. "I have church tomorrow."

"On Wednesday?"

"Yeah. How about we wait till Thursday?"

"Okay. I think the boys will be willing to wait if they know you're going to be here."

"We found it!" Jaycee came charging out of the garage, a plastic bucket swinging from his hand.

"Let's do this." Wesley smiled.

EIGHTEEN

Christopher stomped his feet on the mudroom rug, dislodging the remnants of snow stuck to his boots. Judy opened the door for him the moment she noticed his arms bulging with firewood.

"This ought to keep us warm tonight. I'll fill up the wood box again in the morning." He set the bundle of logs on the floor beside the woodstove, situated several logs on top of the burning coals inside the fireplace, then closed the door and turned the damper down. It would keep until the roosters awakened.

"You and Wesley brought in quite a bit of timber from the woods last summer. Maybe next year the boys can help."

Christopher's bushy eyebrow rose. "Brighton and Jaycee?"

"I have a feeling they might become a permanent fixture around here."

"You mean if Shannon and Wesley get together?"

"Or something else."

His brow furrowed. Sometimes he wished his *fraa* would just come out and say what was on her mind. "What are you talking about, *fraa*?"

"Well, if the government people want to take them away from Shannon—"

"Take them away?"

Judy nodded. "She mentioned that they'd stopped by the house a few times. She sounded worried to me. If that does happen, how would you feel about adopting them?"

"But they're *Englisch*."

"*Der Herr* did not call us to only care for the Plain people, ain't so? We're supposed to look after widows and orphans. And those *kinner* are orphans. *Der Herr* brought them into our life for a reason. That could be the reason."

"Now, *fraa*. You don't think you're wanting those *kinner* because they remind you of our own, do you?"

"That's nonsense. And you wouldn't mind having them here just as much as me."

"You have a point. But I don't know if this is something that would be approved. Besides, I think you need to go through special training to adopt *kinner*."

"Well, I think we should talk to Shannon about it."

"We can talk to her. But I still don't know if it will be approved by the *g'may*."

"I don't see why it wouldn't. And who knows, we might not even have to go through special training. Not if Shannon signs the *kinner* directly over to us."

"She's awfully attached to those *kinner*, especially the *boppli*. She wouldn't give them up unless it was her last hope."

"Well, she could still be just as much a part of their lives as she is now. As a matter of fact, she could move here with us too. We certainly would not exclude her."

"I don't think—"

"Why don't we *chust* pray about it, *schatzi*?"

"Pray, *jah*. Because I don't always know how to deal with my *fraa's ferhoodled* ideas."

"Your *fraa's ferhoodled* ideas? Who is it that lets Jaycee prattle on about Santa? And then encourages him by pretending to see reindeer in the woods."

"*Fraa*, you know that I really did see a deer in our woods. And you can't fault the boy. Especially since we have that red sleigh out in the barn. And our phone shanty *does* kind of look like one of those little houses where the *kinner* take pictures with Santa."

"I'm beginning to worry about you, *schatzi*."

Christopher chuckled. "It wouldn't be the first time, for sure and certain."

"No, it would not."

When Wesley walked into church, he expected curious looks from his brothers and sisters in Christ after the conversation he'd had with his parents. But nobody looked at him or treated him differently. Had Holly blown the whole thing out of proportion so his parents would overreact?

His eyes roamed the fellowship hall until they zeroed in on Holly. She met his gaze and threw her hand in the air. He gestured for her to meet him outside. She followed him, then sat down on the bench next to where he now sat. She was too close, so he scooted over.

She seemed excited. "I didn't know that you were a father. And about you and Shannon. Are you two planning to get married?"

He gritted his teeth, but forced himself to reply calmly. "Neither Shannon nor I have a baby."

"But I—"

"You were being a busybody and Shannon wanted

to put you in your place."

She gasped.

"Listen, Holly. Shannon has not been in church her whole life. As a matter of fact, that was her first time visiting here. She just got saved on Monday. With that being the case, I *really* wish you would have been a better example to her."

Holly frowned at his reprimand.

"As Christians, we shouldn't be gossiping about other people. Please stop. And please quit staring. It's rude." This was the first time he'd outright rebuked a sister in Christ, but it needed to be done. It wasn't his intention to be harsh.

She swallowed and nodded. "I'm sorry."

"I forgive you. But I think you should probably apologize to Shannon next time you see her."

"Is she going to be coming to church here now?"

"I hope so." He rose from the bench. "Thank you for hearing me out. I hope you and Shannon can eventually become friends."

"Okay."

He began walking away, then turned back around. "And Holly, I'm sure God's got someone special for you too."

Her face clouded with emotion. "Thank you for saying that."

A moment later, as he sat down in the pew, Wesley briefly closed his eyes. He prayed things would go well with Holly, then thanked God for His goodness.

NINETEEN

esley, Shannon, and the children pulled onto his grandparents' property from the back side like Wesley always did. He'd been jazzed about this date all day and could think of little else. His work day had been absolutely worthless. He'd sat and daydreamed. All. Day. Long.

If he was like this when and if he ever decided to get married, he and his wife would be homeless and living on the streets. Of course, if he was married, his daydreams would become reality and he'd have no reason to sit and stare out the window all day. He really shouldn't have allowed his fanciful daydreams, but they were too wonderful to dispel.

"I can't wait to see Santa!" Jaycee bounded out of the truck. "Do you think he'll take us for a ride in his sleigh?"

"I think there might be enough snow to build a

snowman." Brighton seemed just as excited to be there as Jaycee.

"Judy!" Melanie squealed as the object of her admiration headed toward the truck.

Wesley chuckled and glanced at Shannon. "It looks like they've already forgotten all about us."

Shannon laughed. "It doesn't look like they'll miss us at all."

Grandma came near and scooped little Melanie into her arms. "I plan to make some special treats with the *kinner*."

Wesley smiled, knowing their Christmas tradition. "Taffy?"

Grandma nodded.

He shared a look with Shannon. "The boys will love it. Especially if you tell them it will help their muscles grow."

"Well, it worked for you, didn't it?" Grandma teased.

Shannon grasped his upper arm and winked. "I think it did."

He shook his head, but loved the teasing nevertheless.

"Your *grossdawdi* and I would like to have a talk with Shannon, if you can spare her a few moments."

He pinned his gaze on Shannon. "You're not starving, are you? We don't have reservations, but there could be a bit of a wait, if they're busy."

"No, I'm fine. I had a snack when I came home from work." She smiled. "Unless you're really hungry."

"I'm good." Although he *was* famished for time alone with her. But he wouldn't ever say anything like that, especially in his grandmother's company. He'd be reprimanded for sure. They'd have to watch themselves here, he reminded himself. While they were free to kiss elsewhere, his grandparents had grown up believing that public displays of affection were inappropriate. Not that he'd cross any lines in their presence *or* alone with Shannon, but he certainly wouldn't mind claiming a kiss.

"Do you mind if Wesley's there too?" Shannon asked Grandma.

His heart jumped in his chest. She wanted him with her?

"I wouldn't mind, except I was hoping he'd keep the *kinner* entertained while we talked."

Wesley nodded. "I can do that."

"Just the boys. I don't think this little one understands enough to know what we'd be talking about." Grandma jostled Melanie and looked at Shannon. "We can give her one of the old dolls to play with. She likes those. Always giving them kisses."

"Yes." Shannon smiled and stroked Melanie's

cheek. "One of her favorite things is showing affection. She's a very loving little girl."

Wesley didn't want to hurry his grandmother, but he and Shannon *were* supposed to be on a date, and he was anxious to get it started. "Where are the boys?"

"Probably in the barn with Christopher. You can show them the sleigh and maybe get it ready."

He grimaced. Hopefully, he wouldn't perspire or get his clothes soiled. Hitching up a horse had not been in his plans tonight. "Grandma," He looked down at his clothes. "I don't think I'm dressed for it."

"Have Brighton do it."

"Brighton?" Shannon and Wesley both said in unison.

"*Jah*, he's been helping out your *grossdawdi* quite a bit. He's becoming a regular horseman."

"I don't think…" Shannon's voice trailed off and he read the worry in her eyes. She didn't want Brighton getting injured.

"It's okay. I'll do it," Wesley said. He'd have to be very careful not to ruin his outfit. Normally, he wouldn't mind, but tonight was special. Their first official date. He wanted to smell good, and he hoped everything would go perfectly.

"Come now," Grandma beckoned Shannon. "I'm sure that *gross sohn* of mine is anxious for time alone with his *aldi*."

Wesley watched forlornly as Shannon followed Grandma into the house. He walked toward the barn just as Grandpa walked out, leading the horse with the sleigh rigged up to it. Jaycee and Brighton sat in the sleigh, their smiles evidencing their excitement.

"I told them you'd take them for a quick spin. You up for it?" Grandpa eyed him carefully.

"Sure."

The boys hooted and hollered, while Wesley climbed in. He wasn't a professional, by any means, but he'd learned how to handle a horse and buggy. He watched Grandpa enter the house. Wesley glanced to the boys in the seat behind him. "You ready?"

"Yeah!" They exclaimed.

"Okay." He kissed the air and lightly jostled the reins, just enough so the horse would begin walking.

Shannon sat in Judy and Christopher's living room, wondering exactly what they'd wanted to speak with her about. Whatever it was sounded important since they hadn't wanted the boys to be present.

"Judy mentioned you'd had some government people come by to see about the *kinner's* welfare."

Christopher glanced at little Melanie in his wife's arms.

"That's right." Where was this conversation going?

Judy leaned forward. "We were thinking. If something were to happen, that if they wanted to take the *kinner* away for some reason. We were thinking that we could take them into our home."

"To adopt them," Christopher clarified. "If you would want that."

"Oh." She frowned. But wait. They were willing to adopt her siblings if she couldn't raise them? She looked into their kind faces. They were so sweet and sincere.

"We would treat them as our own *kinner*," Judy added.

"I'm sure you would." Shannon smiled. "That's a very generous offer. I really appreciate it. But I hope it won't ever come to that."

"Well, just know that they have a place to come, if they need to."

"You two have been so kind to us. I don't know how I'll ever repay you."

Christopher adamantly shook his head. "Repay? *Nee*, we do not expect or want any payment. *Der Herr* has placed this in our hearts."

"Of course, *you* would be welcomed here too." Judy smiled.

"Thank you. It's good to know that I have a place for them, if that were ever to happen." She glanced at little Melanie, who babbled to her baby doll. "But I'm pretty sure it's not a big concern. They said they try to keep families together if at all possible. We're definitely not rich, but we're getting by. I was worried about Christmas, but Wesley told me about a special program at his church where they buy gifts for families who are struggling. I think we'll be okay. Between what you two are doing, helping out with Melanie, and what Wesley has been doing, it's really taken a load off my shoulders. I feel so blessed to have met you all."

"And your family has been a blessing to us. We love having you all here." Judy glanced briefly at Christopher. "You know, your siblings remind us of ours when they were little." Shannon heard the affection in her voice.

"I thought there was only Wesley's father, who is excommunicated, right?"

Christopher nodded. "James is our oldest. He had two younger siblings. They died in a buggy accident when they were *chust kinner*."

"Oh." Shannon's heart filled with compassion. "I'm so sorry. I'm sure that was difficult."

"We accept it as *Gott's* will." Christopher reached over and lightly touched his wife's hand. It was a rare gesture of affection, from what she'd seen of the couple so far.

"It was really hard for us when my parents died. I'd give just about anything to have them back."

"We must not wish for what we cannot have. It will only make us miserable. It is best to accept our circumstances and move on to brighter days."

"I know I have brighter days now because of you and Wesley. It's strange to think that I probably never would have met you, had my parents not died."

"*Der Herr* knows what we need and when we need it. And He brings special people into our lives."

"I think that's what He's done in letting us meet."

Judy smiled. "We feel the same way. These *kinner* fill a hole in our hearts, or at the least, put salve on the hole that is there."

"I'm glad. Having you watch Melanie has been a blessing."

"We are happy to do it."

TWENTY

Wesley pulled his truck to the edge of his grandparents' property and moved the gearshift into Park.

Shannon smiled, her eyes dancing with curiosity. "What are we doing?"

He eyed her from the driver's seat. "You're way too far away from me. Sit by me?" He patted the place next to him on the bench seat.

She nodded and slid over, then fastened the middle seatbelt around her waist.

He slipped his arm around her shoulders, but stopped short of kissing her. Even though he wanted to. Badly. "Much better."

"You're cute." She giggled.

"I think *you're* cute."

She shook her head. "It's hard to believe Christmas is just around the corner."

Change of subject. A perfect distraction from his wayward thoughts.

"Just a little over two weeks." He nodded and maneuvered the truck out onto the road then headed toward Madison. "Oh, yeah. I went ahead and signed the kids up for the Christmas Project at church. I talked to the boys and asked them what they wanted for Christmas. I didn't give anything away, though. It was a pretty general inquiry."

"Thank you for doing that. They will be thrilled."

"I didn't know what to put down for Melanie, so I asked for a doll. I hope that's okay."

"A doll is perfect."

"Okay, I hoped so. Is there anything they're in need of, clothing-wise? I think they like to get them one thing they want and something they need."

"That's really nice. Um…" She blew out a breath. "I guess they can always use socks."

"No jackets or anything? I know how quickly we grew out of our clothes growing up."

"I bought them new jackets when we went school shopping with the money my aunt sent. But Brighton does need a pair of athletic shoes. He said his were too small. I was going to check out the thrift store."

"Okay, shoes. Could Jaycee use some too?"

"Sure. Or maybe put down snow boots for Jaycee?"

"That'll work. I'll need you to write down their sizes for me."

"I can do that."

"Do you think you and the kids can come over on Christmas morning for breakfast? Mom always cooks up a big meal, complete with chocolate gravy and biscuits." He could almost taste them now.

"*Chocolate* gravy?" Her lips twisted. "I've never heard of that."

"Oh, it's the best. The boys will absolutely love it."

"I think I will too. I love chocolate. It does sound a little weird though."

"I think it's a southern thing. My mom's family originated from Arkansas and Oklahoma. It's pretty popular there. I've heard there are even restaurants that serve it."

"Really?"

He nodded. "Chocolate gravy and biscuits for breakfast is one of my favorite family Christmas traditions. Does your family have any?"

"We did." She frowned as though reliving a painful memory.

"You don't have to talk about it if it's too hard. The last thing I want is to make you cry on our date."

"It's okay. I'll try not to." She took a deep breath. "Dad would take the boys out to buy a tree. Not a fresh one from a tree farm, but just from the store. We would all decorate it when they got home. My parents would buy a special ornament for each of us every year." She brushed away a tear. "Sorry."

"No. I don't mind if you cry, I just didn't want you to be sad."

"Well, they're good memories."

"What do you say if we stop by the store after dinner and pick out an ornament for each of the kids?"

She shook her head. "I couldn't ask you to do that, Wesley. You've already done so much."

"I want to. Besides, you want to keep the tradition alive, right?"

"Wesley, are you *sure* you're real? Because I'm seriously having doubts. The last week and a half seem like I've been walking through a dream."

"I'm real." He leaned over and kissed her cheek just before pulling into the parking lot. "Now, are you ready for some delicious seafood?"

"It sounds so good."

"Just wait."

Was swooning really a thing?

Because Shannon was pretty sure she was on the

verge of it right now.

As a matter of fact, if Wesley got the notion to ask her to marry him, she would. Right now. No questions asked.

Was she crazy? Probably.

If Wesley was a dream, she didn't ever want to wake up. And if he was real, she wouldn't be able to bear it if he ever broke up with her. Because she was quite certain that no man would ever—like in a million years—measure up to him.

He opened the truck's door and offered his hand to help her out. She slid off the bench seat and straight into his arms. He leaned down to kiss her and...

"Ow." She laughed. "I hate static electricity."

"I guess my kisses are just too electrifying." He chuckled.

"Shocking, really." She laughed.

"Let's try that again with a little less zing." He brought her close and met her lips with his, then pulled back way too soon for her liking. He looked into her eyes like he wanted more.

Yeah, she did too.

His brow rose as he caressed her cheek with his thumb. "We can continue that later."

She nodded.

"Good." He winked, then reached for her hand. "Let's go eat."

TWENTY-ONE

Wesley knew Key West Shrimp House had been a good choice the moment Shannon first tasted her entrée. She'd closed her eyes in pleasure, or maybe it had been pure ecstasy, when the empty forkful of stuffed cod left her lips. Not that he'd been staring at her lips.

"This." She pointed to her plate and smiled before taking another bite.

He didn't need any more words. He understood perfectly. Which was why this was one of his favorite places to eat in town.

He never could decide if Key West Shrimp House was his favorite or Harry's Stone Grill. He supposed he enjoyed them equally. They both had delicious food and charming, although distinct, atmospheres. Key West was like dining near the sea, whereas Harry's felt more like a rustic hunting cabin—especially with the unique woodwork and taxidermic specimens displayed. He'd be taking her there on their next date night.

He'd spoil her, for sure, but treating her to the best brought him immense pleasure. Especially watching her reaction right now. If anyone deserved to be treated like a princess, Shannon did. And he intended to do just that.

"I'm glad you're enjoying it." He grinned, digging into his own plate.

"They must hire professional chefs here. This is so much better than where I work." She laughed. "Don't tell my boss I said that."

He didn't know if they had professional chefs or not, but it wouldn't surprise him one bit. "My lips are sealed." He zipped his lips for effect. "To be fair though, your restaurant is more of a small family diner."

"True."

"And they don't charge 'chef' prices."

"You have a point."

"Both are necessary and appreciated around here, I think."

"You're right." She glanced at one of the servers, then leaned toward Wesley. "I can't imagine what the waitresses get in tips here. Maybe I should apply." She spoke in a quiet tone.

"You could. Although I'd suspect the majority of customers would come in the evening."

"I didn't think about that." She grimaced. "Yeah, that wouldn't work then. I want to be home when the kids are. As it is, I hate leaving Melanie. I do feel a lot better, though, now that your grandparents are the ones watching her. She loves Judy."

"I'm happy that's working out."

"You know, they offered to adopt the kids if DCS threatened to take them. That's what they wanted to talk to me about before we left."

He frowned. "Really?"

"I thought it was sweet." She stared at him. "Why do you have that look on your face?"

He shrugged. "It's just surprising to me, that's all."

"Why?"

"Well, I guess because my dad is shunned. They never even really made an effort to get to know my brother and me. The only reason they know me now is because I reached out, started visiting them."

"Oh. Really? That's sad."

He nodded, suppressing his emotions. "I guess I never really understood that part of the Amish culture."

"You haven't asked them about it?"

"It's one of those things nobody likes to talk about. I think they feel like it's easier to forget about my dad if they don't think about him."

"That's…terrible. He's their son."

"I know. My dad said they teach that if a person is born Amish and doesn't stay Amish, they are destined for Hell."

"But that's not right, is it?"

"No. Being Amish has nothing to do with salvation. The word Amish isn't even in the Bible. The Amish church wasn't even started until the sixteen hundreds. The *only* thing our salvation rests upon is Jesus Christ. But trying to teach that to a religious group that has been steeped in hundreds of years of tradition is like trying to teach a cow to sing."

"But you've tried?"

"To teach a cow to sing?" he teased.

She shook her head.

"Yeah, I've tried talking to them. But I'm praying that God will open a door and open their hearts to His truth. I want them to be saved. They are truly wonderful people." He raised a sad smile. "But wonderful people don't go to Heaven, true believers do."

"Maybe…do you think us coming into their lives might open a door?"

"It would be wonderful if it did. That's why I was surprised that they took to your family so readily. Normally, the Amish keep to themselves and don't mingle much with the *Englisch*. Maybe this is a sign that their hearts are beginning to open."

"I hope that's the case."

He reached across the table for her hand. "I'm glad you've come into all our lives. You and the kids have brought joy to my heart."

Her eyes widened. "We have?"

"Very much so." And hopefully they would for many years to come. But he wouldn't say that out loud.

He glanced down at her food. "Are you going to need a to-go box?"

"I think so."

Christopher chuckled as he sat on the dining bench he'd made. Watching the smiles on these *kinner's* faces as they pulled taffy brought joy to his own heart. Oh, how he missed the times when his and Judy's *kinner* were little. The times before the accident that took their lives. The times before James had forsaken his Amish heritage.

"Will you come to school with me one day?" Jaycee's grin stretched across his face.

"School?" Christopher's brow jumped and he glanced at his *fraa*. "Ain't been to school in a really long time."

"Pleeeaaase? None of the kids believe me when I tell them that Santa babysits my little sister. I want them to see you."

Christopher chuckled.

"You don't even have to wear your red suit or nothin'."

"Don't know if Prancer would make it all the way to your school. It's quite a ways away."

Jaycee frowned and hung his head. "Aww…"

He hated disappointing the little guy.

An idea popped into his head. "But maybe I can see you off on the bus one morning." He knew he really shouldn't encourage the boy's fantasies, but he couldn't help enjoying the smile it brought to his face. If he could make the boy smile, he would.

"For reals? You would do that?" Jaycee's excitement shown in his entire countenance.

He nodded. "Just tell me when."

Judy met his gaze, then shook her head. You'd think with all the things she'd had to put up with over the years, she'd be used to his *ferhoodled* ideas. But perhaps this one took the cake.

He shot a wink in her direction, reached for a piece

of unwrapped taffy, then popped it into his mouth with a smile.

"Time to clean up now! Your sister and Wesley should be here at any moment." Christopher glanced up at the clock. A quarter till eight. His *gross sohn* said they planned to be back around eight.

"Aww...do we have to go home?" Jaycee complained.

"I heard you were supposed to be decorating a tree tonight. Don't want to miss that, do you?" Christopher said the words, but didn't understand why *Englischers* did all the silly things they did. Of course, he didn't reckon *Englischers* understood their traditions either.

"I almost forgot!" Jaycee jumped up and down. "Do you want to come help us decorate it? I can ask Shannon to make you some cookies! I think we have milk too."

"No, thank you." Christopher chuckled. He couldn't even imagine decorating a tree. Jaycee's fanciful notions were over the top.

Just as he suspected, Wesley's knock sounded on the back door.

"It's Shannon and Wesley! I'll get it!" Jaycee raced

to the door before Christopher could even think to protest.

Jaycee threw the door open. "You're here! You're here!"

Wesley caught his eye. His gaze moved to their intertwined hands, then Wesley broke the connection. He didn't really mind that they were holding hands, but Wesley must've believed that was the case. Perhaps his father had shared stories with him.

"Did you have a good time?" Shannon walked in ahead of Wesley at his insistence.

Jaycee bounced. "The best! Wait until you taste the taffy we made. And guess what? Santa said he was going to come to the bus stop with me and wave to my friends!"

Wesley and Shannon both looked at Christopher in surprise.

He shrugged. "I couldn't say no." He chuckled.

"Are we still going to decorate the tree tonight?" Brighton spoke up.

"Yep. Are you guys all ready to go?" Wesley asked.

Judy walked into the main room, a bag of taffy in her hands.

"Wow! It looks like you were busy." Wesley smiled at the children.

"Yeah, my arms are tired." Brighton grinned.

"You should see how big our muscles are now!" Jaycee proclaimed.

Christopher couldn't help but laugh.

"We need to get going if we're going to decorate the tree," Shannon said. She turned to look at him and Judy. "Thank you so much for watching them for me."

"For us," Wesley chimed in.

"They were a joy." Judy smiled.

"I hope they didn't give you any trouble." Shannon worried her lip.

"No trouble at all," Christopher said.

"Hey." Wesley pulled him and Judy to the side, his voice low. "Would you guys like to come with us on Saturday? We're going to take the kids to see the Christmas lights at the Creation Museum."

"Saturday, you say?" Christopher scratched his head. Did that date sound familiar? He looked at Judy.

"*Nee*, we're going to the auction, remember?"

Of course. How could he forget the auction? They didn't usually have them this time of year, but a need had come up.

"Okay." Wesley's enthusiasm faded just a bit. "Maybe next time."

He hated to say no to their *gross sohn*, but they'd already made plans. "I'm sure you will have a *gut* time without us," he assured.

"Maybe you can join our family on Christmas morning for breakfast, then?" His tone was hopeful, but not confident. He likely already knew the answer.

"You know we cannot."

Wesley sighed in disappointment. "Okay, then."

Shannon gathered the children then asked Wesley if he was ready. Wesley hugged both him and Judy, then said goodbye.

Christopher waved from the door as the group of *kinner* all made their way to his *gross sohn's* truck. He would have walked out with them, but he didn't wish to slow them down since they'd been anxious to get home.

He turned to Judy after they'd driven away. "They are going to make a nice family, ain't so?"

"*Jah*. Wesley will be a *gut dat* to those *kinner*."

He eyed his *fraa*. "How long do you think it will be before they get hitched?"

"It was two years for us."

"I can't see those two waiting two years. That *bu* can hardly contain himself now." He chuckled. "I remember the feeling. I'm *chust* glad I don't have to anymore."

He leaned down and kissed his *fraa* on the cheek.

TWENTY-TWO

"Jaycee, stop putting tinsel on Melanie's head. That's not okay." Shannon put her hand on her hip and huffed, shaking her head at Jaycee and his shenanigans.

"But she likes it, see?" He put another string of tinsel on Melanie's head and she giggled.

Shannon stopped her baby sister just before she put the tinsel into her mouth. "No, baby."

She turned back to Jaycee. "*That's* why I don't want you to do that."

"Aww…"

"You need to listen to Shannon. She's older and she knows what's best." Wesley spoke up.

"But she's not Mom," he protested.

"It's true that she didn't give birth to you, but she's the closest thing you have to a mom right now. You need to obey her and do what she says," Wesley insisted.

"Okay," Jaycee said glumly.

Shannon mouthed a *thank you* to Wesley.

"Oh! We almost forgot something." Shannon pulled the bag of ornaments, that she and Wesley had purchased earlier, from her purse.

"What is it?" Brighton smiled as he placed one of the last ornaments from the box onto the tree. Shannon loved to see him happy. He'd been the most melancholy of her siblings since their parents' accident.

"Wesley and I got something for you guys." She pulled the ornaments from the bag and handed them to Wesley to do the honors.

"Is it a candy bar?" Jaycee grinned.

Shannon pointed to him. "You, little boy, eat too much candy."

"Uh uh." He shook his head. "Judy only let me have seven pieces of taffy."

"Seven pieces?" Shannon frowned. "Jaycee. If you don't stop eating so much sugar, you're going to get a toothache."

"You sound like Mom."

Wesley nodded to prove his prior point. He then handed an ornament to each of the boys.

Jaycee held up his ornament. "It's a sleigh, just like Santa's!"

Shannon knew he'd get a kick out of that. It had been Wesley's idea.

Brighton's reaction to his basketball ornament was a little more subdued and she wondered if he was thinking of Mom and Dad. "Thank you, Wesley."

"I have something for you too." Wesley's smile glistened next to the lights on the Christmas tree.

"For me?" She grinned as he handed her something wrapped in tissue paper. "When did you…?"

"Just open it," he urged.

She pulled out a heart-shaped ornament. The message on it read, "I love us."

"Oh, Wesley." Her heart soared, but she held her emotions back. "This…you are the best."

She took two steps forward and rewarded him with a kiss. "I love us too."

"I was hoping for that reaction." He murmured and kissed her again before letting her go.

"What about Melanie? Doesn't she get one too?" Jaycee asked.

"She sure does." Shannon pulled Melanie close and handed her a bag. "Open it, baby."

"Baby!" Melanie pulled out her ornament. "Baby Jesus!"

Shannon gasped and looked at Wesley. "How did she know that?"

He shrugged.

"Let's put Baby Jesus on the tree."

"No, no." She held the ornament close to her heart, hugging it. "My Baby Jesus."

Shannon laughed.

"I don't think she's going to surrender willingly." Wesley laughed.

"I guess she likes it." Shannon looked at the boys. "Okay, it's way past your bedtime and you two have school tomorrow."

"Ah…can't we skip school tomorrow?" Jaycee pouted.

"No. Bed. And make sure to do a good job brushing your teeth." Shannon pointed to the hallway, then looked at Wesley. "He's in kindergarten and he already wants to skip school."

The boys reluctantly obeyed, and Shannon tucked Melanie in. The precious baby had already been half asleep, with her ornament clutched to her chest, before Shannon pulled the blanket over her. She'd sleep like a rock tonight.

Shannon would no doubt sleep well too. She'd been going since early that morning. She yawned as she walked back into the living room and joined Wesley on the couch. The lights from the Christmas tree twinkled as they cycled off and on.

She stared at the Christmas tree and sighed. "It's so pretty."

"That was fun." Wesley slipped his arm around her and she snuggled close to him.

"Are you as tired as I am?"

"Probably not. You look pretty worn out." He smoothed her hair with his hand, then lifted her chin. His kiss was slow and gentle and everything wonderful.

She could stay like that forever. Right there, nestled in Wesley's strong arms, listening to the steady beat of his heart.

"I should let you get some sleep now." He murmured into her temple, kissing it in the process.

"I wish you didn't have to go. Ever."

He caressed her cheek, then gazed into her eyes. "That's exactly how I feel. But I *should* go."

She reluctantly moved so he could stand up from the couch. "Thank you for tonight, Wesley. It was a lot of fun."

"Speaking of fun, I was thinking of leaving around six on Saturday to go to the Creation Museum. Will that work for you?" He walked toward the door.

"Six sounds good. I'm looking forward to it."

He pulled her close and kissed her one last time. Emotion warred in his eyes. "I'm falling helplessly in love with you, Shannon Parker." He grazed her forehead with his lips, then stepped out the door.

Shannon was nearly ready for bed when a knock sounded at the door. *Wesley?* Maybe he'd forgotten something.

It was times like this she wished her door had a peephole. She pulled the door open.

Her eyes widened. "Aiden? What are you doing here?"

He stepped into the house without invitation.

"It's wonderful to see you too, Shan." His voice was louder than usual. Had he been drinking? One whiff of his breath told her that her assumptions had been correct.

She wanted to tell him to go home, but she couldn't imagine him driving anywhere in his current state. "Why are you here?"

She closed the door, denying the frigid air entrance.

"You haven't been answering my phone calls or texts." His voice was still loud.

"Keep it down. The kids are asleep." She reprimanded in a forceful whisper. "I *did* answer them, remember? I told you that our relationship was over and to stop trying to contact me. I have another boyfriend now."

"Aw, Shan. Don't be like that."

"Aiden, you're drunk. How did you get here?"

He held up his keys and jingled them in his hand.

She rolled her eyes, then took his keys from him.

She'd have taken him home if the children hadn't been in bed already, but that wasn't an option now. She could suggest he sleep in his car but it was really cold outside. She sighed.

"Okay. You're not going anywhere tonight. I'll get a blanket for you and you can sleep on the couch."

He reached for her, but she stepped out of the way. "You gonna join me?"

"No. Now take off your shoes and go lie down."

"You're bossy."

"I know. I'm also tired. Now, if you don't want to sleep in your car tonight, I suggest you do as I say."

"Aw, Shan. I can drive home. Or we could go on a date."

"I'm not going on any more dates with you. And you're certainly not driving anywhere." She took him by the arm and led him to the couch. "Now, go to sleep."

As soon as he sat on the couch, Shannon went to retrieve a blanket from the hall closet. Aiden was already out by the time she returned to the living room. She sighed in blessed relief and covered him with the blanket before heading off to bed herself.

Christopher knocked on the Parkers' door the following morning. He couldn't wait to see Jaycee's face light up when he saw that he'd kept his promise to see him off on the school bus this morning. He'd even brought a box of candy canes to give to Jaycee so he could distribute them to his friends.

To his surprise, a shirtless young man opened the door. Christopher's jaw dropped. Who was this young man and why was he here?

"May I help you?" The young man's tone was rude.

Christopher's brow furrowed. "Who are you? And why are you here?"

"I'm Shannon's boyfriend and I spent the night. Any more questions that are none of your business, old man?"

Somebody needed to put this young man in his place. But...*Shannon's boyfriend? Spent the night?* Hadn't she been with his *gross sohn* just last night?

"Is Jaycee here?"

"Yeah." The young man closed the door, leaving him out in the cold.

A moment later, the door swung open and he was greeted with Jaycee's wide grin. "Santa!" The boy threw his arms around his legs. "You came."

Warmth radiated through Christopher, almost enough to forget his rude welcome this morning. "You ready?"

"Yep." He turned around and hollered into the

house. "Brighton, let's go! Santa's here."

Shannon poked her head out of the kitchen and waved. "Did you remember your lunch, Jaycee?"

He held up an insulated lunch container. "Right here."

"You be good," she told Jaycee. Her eyes moved to Christopher. "I'll drop off Melanie in just a little bit."

"You'll probably be there before I get home."

"Okay. Thanks for doing this for Jaycee."

He nodded, waved then stepped out the door with the boys.

It was only a short walk to their bus stop and Jaycee chatted the entire way. The boy was a burst of sunshine. Before Jaycee left his side, Christopher had given him the box of candy canes. Jaycee hugged him, then literally bounced onto the school bus.

Jaycee and his smiling friends all waved with their candy canes as the bus drew away from the curb.

He was certain Jaycee would have a wonderful day and he was happy he could be a small part of it.

Wesley, on the other hand, was a different story. Christopher would need to make a phone call to his *gross sohn* to see what exactly was going on. Had he and Shannon broken up sometime between last night and this morning? It didn't seem possible, as happy as they'd been, but who knew?

Nevertheless, he'd speak to Wesley.

TWENTY-THREE

Wesley's phone vibrated in his pocket and he reached to see who it was. He glanced down at the number. The phone shanty? Why would Grandma or Grandpa be calling this early in the morning? Hopefully nothing was wrong.

He tapped to answer the call. "Hello?"

"Wesley?"

"Hello, Grandpa. Is everything okay?"

"I'm not sure." He heard the concern in Grandpa's voice.

"What's going on? Are you and Grandma watching Melanie? Is she okay?"

"*Jah*, she is fine." He paused. "Did you and your *aldi* have a fight last night?"

"A fight? No. Shannon and I are great." Why had Grandpa asked that? "Is…why do you ask?"

Grandpa's heavy sigh came through the phone. "I

195

don't want to be the bearer of bad news, but I think your *aldi* might be cheating on you."

His heart clenched. No, that wasn't possible. Was it? "Grandpa, why are you saying this? Did you hear something?"

"*Nee*, I saw it with my own eyes."

He would not get upset. He would not panic. "Saw what? What did you see, Grandpa?" Did he really want to know?

"I stopped by the *haus* this morning to see Jaycee off on the school bus. A young man opened the door. He said he was Shannon's beau. He said he spent the night."

"Spent the...*what*?" His heart raced. No, this wasn't Shannon. Not his Shannon. There had to be a good explanation. There *had* to be.

"He answered the door without a shirt on. I'm pretty sure he was telling the truth. He looked like he'd recently awakened."

This was unbelievable! "Are you sure you were at the right house?"

"Oh, I'm sure. Jaycee and Brighton left with me. I saw Shannon too."

"You saw Shannon? What did she say? Did you talk to her?"

"She was in the kitchen. She seemed happy. I *chust* said hello."

His hand raked through his hair. "Who was it? Was it Aiden?"

"I don't think he said his name, *chust* introduced himself as Shannon's beau."

"Is there anything else you can tell me?"

"*Nee*, that's it. I *chust* thought you'd want to know. I don't want to think ill of your *aldi*, but…"

Yeah, neither did he. "Okay, thanks for letting me know, Grandpa."

He clicked off the phone. He hadn't planned on making a trip into town today, but now it seemed inevitable. He could text or call Shannon, but he really needed to see her in person. He needed reassurance.

Shannon had just served a platter of food to the customer at the counter when Wesley walked into the restaurant. She was happy to see him, but her smile faltered when she noticed his concerned expression. Hopefully nothing was wrong.

"Hey." She smiled as she moved past him with a platter in her hand. "Be right back."

She glanced over her shoulder and saw him plant himself in his usual spot. She set Aiden's food down in front of him and he smiled up at her. "Thanks for everything, Shan. Are you sure you won't reconsider?"

"I already told you, Aiden. I'm with Wesley."

"He's an idiot."

She frowned. "No, he is not. He's a great guy."

She wondered if Aiden had noticed that Wesley had come into the restaurant. Either way, she needed to get back to him. This was a busy morning and she didn't have time to converse. Especially with Aiden.

She moved back to the counter, her hands empty now. She looked at Wesley. "Coffee?"

He shook his head and frowned. Something was wrong. There had to be something wrong if he refused a cup of coffee.

She stopped in front of him and reached for his hand. "What is it?"

He pulled his hand away. The cold gesture stung more than the biting snow this morning. "Did Aiden spend the night last night?" He wouldn't bring his eyes to hers.

"Yes, he did." She glanced back as the bell dinged, indicating the food was ready.

He stood from the bar stool.

Her heart nearly stopped. "Wesley, don't go."

"You're busy." He glanced at the two plates of food in her hands.

"Yes, I am. But we need to talk. Please stay."

"Hey, Shan." Aiden called from his booth. "This thing's out of ketchup." He held up an empty bottle.

She sighed, but caught the look of hurt in Wesley's eyes. "It's not what you think."

But she couldn't stand there and talk. The customers needed their food. "I'll be right back."

She hurried to one of the booths, dropped off the food, and asked the customers if they'd needed anything else. Aiden could wait for his ketchup.

To her relief, Wesley had sat back down. For a moment, she'd worried that he'd leave. But he didn't strike her as the leaving type, which brought a bit of comfort to her heart.

She grabbed a cup of coffee for him, so she'd have an excuse to talk with him a minute. She set it down in front of him. "Aiden stopped by last night after you left. He'd been drinking. I didn't think it was safe for him to be on the road in his condition. I would have told him to sleep in his car, but it was too cold. I'm sorry, but I didn't know what else to do."

"Why didn't you call me? I would have come back. I could have given him a ride home."

"You were probably halfway home already. I didn't want to bother you. Besides, Aiden's car was at my house."

His jaw worked. "I don't like you being in the house alone with him. I don't trust him."

"I really didn't know what else to do. I was tired and I just wanted to go to sleep."

"Call me next time, okay? Anytime. For any reason. Even if I was already home, I would have come back."

"Okay." Another order came up and she grabbed the bottle of ketchup for Aiden. She quickly took the order to the table, dropped off the ketchup, then checked on her other customers. When she returned, Wesley still sat at the counter drinking his coffee.

He reached for her hand. "I'm sorry I overreacted. Forgive me?"

She couldn't resist his puppy dog eyes. "Okay. But I'm a little concerned that you don't trust me."

"It's him I don't trust." He glanced toward Aiden's table. "Put yourself in my shoes, Shannon. If you showed up at my house in the early morning and saw a pretty young woman dressed in a little nightgown, who you knew was my ex-girlfriend, how would you react?"

She frowned. "I think I'd be upset."

He nodded. "And for good reason. I don't have any business having an ex-girlfriend sleep over, right?"

"You're right. But I would hope that you wouldn't let her drive intoxicated."

"No, I guess if I was in the same situation you were

in, I likely would have done the same thing. But that doesn't mean it still wouldn't have looked bad to others." He stood.

"Are you leaving?"

He shook his head. "Not yet. I have some business to discuss first." He glanced at Aiden.

"Wesley…" She worried her lip.

"Don't worry. I'll be civil." He dug in his pocket and brought out a five-dollar bill, then placed it under his coffee mug.

She noticed a customer with her hand in the air. "I've got work to do. See you on Saturday, then?"

"You bet." He stepped close to kiss her cheek, but must've thought better of it. He squeezed her hand instead. "Don't work too hard."

Wesley slid into the booth across from Aiden.

Aiden frowned. "What are you doing?"

"I want to know what *you're* doing." Wesley's stare was pointed, and dead serious.

"I'm obviously trying to enjoy my breakfast. Last I checked, that wasn't a crime." His sarcasm grated on Wesley's nerves.

"You know that is *not* what I was referring to. I thought I made it clear that I wanted you to stay away from Shannon."

"And I want a billion dollars. We don't always get what we want, do we?" He had the audacity to smirk.

Wesley's fists clenched. He wanted to knock this guy into next Thursday so badly he could taste it. But he'd promised Shannon he'd be civil and he planned to keep that promise. "If you continue to bother her, I will get a restraining order."

"Listen, *Lesley*. Or whatever your name is. This is a free country. If I want to visit Shannon here or at her house, I'm going to. Go ahead and try to get a restraining order. They won't give you one." His annoying laugh almost undid Wesley's resolve.

Wesley needed to walk away right now, because if he didn't, this guy was going to get seriously hurt. His nonresistance roots ran deep, but not that deep. It took everything in him to slide out of the booth and walk away.

"That's what I thought." Aiden laughed.

Wesley ignored him, although every fiber in his being wanted to retaliate. But he was a better man than that. He would not let this jerk take control over his thoughts.

He did, however, need to have a chat with Shannon.

As soon as she moved to the register, he met her there. "Will you call me as soon as you get off work?"

"Why?" She glanced toward Aiden's table.

"We need to have a talk. I don't trust that guy. At all."

"What did he say?"

"Well, he has no intention of staying away from you. It might be wise to get a restraining order." Or a gun, because a piece of paper wasn't going to stop a bad guy from doing bad things, if that was what he wished to do.

"I don't know if it would do any good."

"Why wouldn't it? It would at least be a deterrent, right?"

She shrugged. "His dad is a cop."

"*What*?" *Now* things were beginning to make sense. The cop who claimed Wesley had been stalking Shannon. It had to be Aiden's dad. Which meant Aiden was probably the one who'd called in. He likely thought he could get away with whatever he wanted. And he might just be right to a certain extent. *Oh, boy.*

Wesley sighed. "Well, let's just do our part. We can try to ignore him and hope he goes away. If he keeps coming around, I think we should go ahead and file a restraining order. At least then, there will be a paper trail."

"Paper trail? You don't think he'd try to hurt me or the kids, do you?"

"He wants you and he knows he can't have you, yet he's still trying. There have been obsessed ex-boyfriends who have done a lot worse." He glanced toward Aiden's booth again to make sure he was still seated. "Do you own a gun?"

She swallowed. "A gun? I don't…" She shook her head. "Wesley…"

"It's better to be safe than sorry. You're at least ten minutes away from the police station."

"I don't want to have a gun with the kids in the house. I've known Aiden for years. We went to school together. I just don't think he'd do anything like that. Wesley, I think you're overreacting."

"I hope I am, because I would never want anything to happen to you or the kids." He cupped her cheek. "Listen, I need to let you work and I've got to get to work too. Construction job. Call me if you need *anything*, okay?"

She nodded.

He took a deep breath, and walked out of the restaurant and toward his truck. But he wasn't about to leave. Not until Aiden did. He'd circle the block, then park somewhere across the street out of view so he wouldn't look conspicuous.

He didn't trust Aiden, even now more than ever. If his father was a cop… *God, I need Your guidance here.*

Not ten minutes later, Aiden stepped out of the restaurant and drove off. Wesley was tempted to follow him, but he wouldn't. He needed to get to work.

God, please keep Shannon and the children safe.

TWENTY-FOUR

Jaycee had come home from school on Thursday talking about how all his friends really did believe him about Santa now, and they wanted to meet him too. Poor Christopher. Jaycee was turning the Amish man into a local celebrity. Well, among the five-year-old population, at least. Sooner or later, she'd need to sit him down for a serious talk.

Shannon hadn't told the children where they'd be going Saturday, because she'd wanted it to be a surprise. Jaycee was already jazzed enough about everything else going on. It brought a smile to her face just knowing how much the children's spirits had lifted since Wesley and the Stoltz family had come into their lives.

"Are you going to tell us where we're going yet?" Jaycee sang from the backseat of Wesley's truck.

Wesley tapped his fingers on the steering wheel and

looked at Shannon. "Do you think we should tell them?"

"How about after we cross over the bridge into Kentucky?" she suggested.

"We're going all the way to Kentucky?" Jaycee's excitement turned up another notch. "We get to go over a bridge?"

"Yep." Wesley smiled at Shannon.

"Jaycee, Kentucky's not that far away. We've been there before." Brighton informed him.

"When?" Jaycee challenged.

"Remember the pizza place with all the games?" Wesley asked.

"We're going to the pizza place again?" Jaycee bounced.

"No, we're not getting pizza," Shannon said. "Wesley just asked if you *remember* it. Listen to people's words before you answer, please."

"I remember it." Jaycee nodded.

"Well, the pizza place was in Kentucky," Wesley informed him.

"It was?"

Wesley confirmed with a nod.

"Then I like Kentucky!" Jaycee grinned.

"Tucky!" Melanie added her two cents.

Shannon reached back and tickled her tummy. "Oh, you like Kentucky too, huh?"

"You'll like it even better after tonight," Wesley said. "Here comes the bridge!"

They drove over the bridge as the children all bellowed, "River, river, river, river!"

Shannon laughed when Wesley looked at her strangely. She shook her head. "Don't ask."

"Family tradition?" His brow rose.

"Something like that. I think my mom came up with that."

Wesley laughed. "We used to lift our hands and say 'Praise the Lord!' when we drove over railroad tracks."

"Really? So we're not the only weird family then." She smiled.

"Apparently not."

"You have to tell us now!" Jaycee said.

Wesley looked at Shannon, his tone teasing. "We have to tell them something? What are we supposed to tell them again?"

Shannon tapped her chin and played along. "Hmm…I don't know if I can remember what we're supposed to tell them."

Jaycee giggled at their foolishness. "Where we're going, silly!"

"We're going silly? I thought we were already silly." Wesley made a funny face at Shannon and the kids.

Jaycee huffed in exasperation.

"Okay, okay." Wesley stalled and looked at Shannon. "Should you tell them or should I?"

Shannon smiled and shook her head at Wesley's teasing. "We're going to the Creation Museum!"

"A museum?" Brighton didn't look too enthused. "It sounds boring."

"Boring? Now, would Wesley take you to some place boring?" Wesley acted offended.

Brighton shrugged.

"Well, I guess it might be boring." Wesley's shoulders moved. "I mean, if you don't like Christmas lights. And dinosaurs. And planets and stars. And zip lines. And Baby Jesus." He glanced back at little Melanie when he said that.

"Baby Jesus!" Melanie squealed. She'd brought her ornament along with her. It hadn't moved out of her sight since she'd opened it the other night.

"Dinosaurs? For reals?" Jaycee jumped up and down. It was amazing his seat belt stayed fastened. Maybe Shannon should give the company a five-star review online, because if it could contain Jaycee, it could contain just about anything.

"You will *love* the planetarium," Wesley assured. "I hope it's open tonight. If not, we'll have to come back another time."

"What's a planetarium?" Brighton asked.

"It's like a theater, where you recline back in chairs, and they show a video on the ceiling telling you all about the universe. It's pretty impressive."

The children's chatter had settled down to a low hum in the backseat as Brighton and Jaycee discussed the Creation Museum between themselves.

Shannon's heart soared with love for this man beside her. There was nothing about him she didn't love. He was thoughtful. Caring. Imaginative. And he apparently loved her siblings just as much as she did. She couldn't imagine him not being in their lives now.

But loving meant losing, right? If she got too close to Wesley, one day she'd have to let him go. Just like Mom and Dad. And she couldn't bear the thought of *ever* losing Wesley. Her heart throbbed at just the possibility.

Wesley reached over and rubbed her upper arm. "What are you thinking?"

She shook her head. "I'll tell you later."

"You sure?"

She nodded.

TWENTY-FIVE

Wesley turned into the parking lot of the Creation Museum and paid the small fee to the attendant. The Christmas Town light display was free, but parking was five dollars. Not bad for a night of entertainment for the whole family. And if the kiddos wanted to participate in the things he'd mentioned, he'd happily fork over the money for those activities as well.

This little family had their share of pain and heartache. Since this was their first Christmas without their parents, he wanted to make it as enjoyable as possible.

"I see the Christmas lights!" Jaycee hollered.

Wesley shared a smile with Shannon. There was never a dull moment with Jaycee around.

"Wow, there are a lot of people here," Brighton remarked.

As he pulled the truck into a parking space, Shannon turned around and addressed the children. "These are the rules. We need to stay together. If you need to use the restroom or want to see something special, you need to be with either me or Wesley. There's no going off by yourselves. And don't talk to strangers. Got it?"

The children agreed.

Shannon turned to Wesley. "We need to get Mel's stroller out of the back." Then she looked at the boys. "Don't forget your jackets, scarves, and hats. It looks like it's cold out there."

"We ready?" Wesley was anxious for them to discover everything the Creation Museum had to offer.

"Let's do this." Shannon rubbed her hands together and opened the door before he had a chance to jog around the truck and open it for her. He let the boys out of the back instead.

A few moments later, they walked toward the entrance. Shannon pushed the stroller containing Melanie, while Wesley walked alongside the boys.

"Whoa-ho-ho-ho! Check out that dinosaur, Brighton!" Jaycee ran straight to the large sculpture and examined it from the ground up. It must've been huge to the little guy. "That's super cool! You were right, Wesley. It's not boring at all."

He got a kick out of seeing things through Jaycee's

eyes. He couldn't even remember when everything was new and exciting. Except for meeting Shannon maybe. He glanced over at her as she squatted down next to the stroller and pointed the dinosaur out to Melanie. Her entire countenance glowed. She was truly beautiful inside and out. Yeah, she was exciting alright.

"You ready to go see the lights?" Wesley prompted.

"Lights!" Melanie clapped her mitten-clad hands, still clinging to her ornament.

During the next hour, they explored the lights, listened as the shepherds proclaimed the Saviour's birth and the scribes talked about how the promised Messiah had come, according to the prophecies and the rumors on the streets. Melanie's favorite part was Baby Jesus. She'd wanted to get out of her stroller to go give Him kisses.

"Okay, does anyone need to use the restroom before we head back home?" Shannon asked the boys.

Wesley suspected they would, since they'd indulged in hot cocoa.

"I do," Jaycee said.

"We'll need to walk back inside the building." Wesley instructed. He pulled the keys from his pocket. "If no one else needs to use the restroom, you can head to the truck. I know the little one is getting tired. She'll likely be asleep before we exit the parking lot."

"Okay." She looked at Brighton.

"I'll go with you," he told her.

Wesley watched as they walked toward the truck. When they were out of sight, he and Jaycee headed toward the restroom. Wesley waited outside the door, since the bathroom seemed quite populated. "I'll just be right here, okay?"

"Okay," Jaycee hurried inside.

A few minutes later, Wesley and Jaycee headed to the truck to meet the others.

As soon as they were all fastened into the truck, Jaycee exclaimed, "Guess what? I saw Aiden!"

Wesley looked at Shannon. "Where?"

"He was in the bathroom."

"Did you talk to him?" Shannon asked.

"Of course. He's not a stranger."

"What did he say?" Wesley frowned.

"He asked me who I was here with. And he asked me if I liked him or Wesley better." His grin widened. "I told him Wesley."

Wesley chuckled. "I bet he loved that answer," he mumbled.

"Did he ask you anything else?" Shannon asked.

"He asked how long we'd been there and what we were going to do."

Shannon shook her head.

"Sounds like I should have gone in with him." Wesley chided himself.

"You didn't know Aiden was going to be there." Shannon's hand on his was comforting.

"No, he's the last person I expected to see here."

"He said he was going home now too," Jaycee volunteered.

Wesley looked at Shannon and frowned. Had Aiden been following them? His eyes scanned the parking lot for any trace of Aiden. He turned the ignition over and backed out of the parking space.

Shannon watched the lights of the car behind them in her rearview side mirror. She couldn't make out what model of vehicle it was, but they seemed to be trailing awfully close. The children had all fallen asleep, but soft Christmas music played in the background of the truck's cab.

"I think we're being followed." She whispered to Wesley, not wanting to wake or worry the kids.

"I know. I'm pretty sure it's Aiden." He grimaced. "He's been behind us the whole time."

"He has? What do you think he wants?"

"You. He wants you, Shannon." His tone evidenced frustration. "Maybe we should have filed that restraining order already."

"Do you think he'll follow us all the way home?"

"I don't know. But if he does, I'm not leaving you and the kids alone."

"Do you think he's been drinking again?"

"He sure does drive like it. But he might just be trying to intimidate me."

She smiled. "He must not know you very well."

"I don't like him putting you and the kids in danger. He needs to be put in his place." His grip on the steering wheel tightened.

"What are you going to do?"

"I'm tempted to call the police."

"But if Aiden's dad works there…"

"Yeah. My thoughts exactly." He pulled into her driveway, but the car behind them drove past. "Good. I hope he doesn't come back."

Wesley jogged around and quickly opened Shannon's door. "Let's get the kids inside."

They loosed the children from their car seats and headed to the house.

"Okay." She pulled out her keys and fumbled with the lock. She didn't know why she was nervous. It was just Aiden. But he *had* been acting weird lately. And

Wesley's serious tone concerned her. Did he see something she hadn't?

"I'm not leaving. Are you fine with that?" He carried a sleeping Jaycee in his arms. The boy was out like a lantern that had burned all its oil. He hadn't budged.

"I'd feel better if you stayed." She was grateful for his presence. She finally got the door open and Wesley locked the deadbolt behind them. Brighton went straight to his bed without being told. She carried little Melanie to her room, while Wesley tucked Jaycee in.

A moment later, the two of them met back in the living room. Wesley opened his arms and she melted into his protective cocoon, the tension automatically leaving her body as his hands gently massaged her shoulders. She leaned back a little and lifted her chin, conveying with her eyes that she desired Wesley's kiss. He willingly obliged. His lips met hers, moving slowly and surely, as they always did. One of his hands loosely cradled the back of her head while the other caressed her neck just below her ear. She'd come to enjoy the way Wesley kissed. He took delight in every nanosecond they touched, as though each movement brought him immense pleasure. She felt cherished in his arms.

The doorbell rang, startling both of them.

"It's Aiden." She groaned. "Maybe if we ignore him, he'll go away."

"Call the cops, will you? That way we can at least document that he followed us home." The seriousness in his eyes returned.

The doorbell rang several more times in a row. If Aiden didn't stop, he'd awaken the kids.

Wesley walked toward the door. "I'll deal with him. You stay here, okay?"

"Wesley…be careful."

He turned to her before opening the door, caressing her cheek. "I just plan to talk to him," he reassured her.

As soon as Wesley stepped out the door, she picked up her cell phone.

TWENTY-SIX

Wesley stepped out the door, but not before turning the inside lock. Aiden refused to back up, so Wesley moved to the side. He was getting really fed up with Aiden's games.

"What do you want?" Wesley frowned.

"I want to see my girl."

"She's not your girl. And you need to leave. You're disturbing the peace."

Aiden sneered.

"I'm serious. We've already called the police."

"Yeah, right." Aiden's annoying laugh filled the air. He truly believed he was above the law. Or at least untouchable. "Like I told you before, *Lesley*, this is a free country."

"Your freedom ends where another person's begins. You happen to be standing on private property. Uninvited and unwelcomed. I suggest you leave before the cops show up and escort you off the property."

"So I'm guessing Shannon didn't tell you what we did the other night when I slept over."

Did this guy really think he'd believe his foolhardy words? "You need to leave. Right now."

"I'm not going anywhere."

"Fine. Then stand out here in the cold until the cops come get you. I'm going inside where it's warm." He turned, poised to knock on the door, but stopped short when something slammed against his upper back and his head, the force knocking him off his feet. His head throbbed and pain shot through his back. He glanced up in time to see Aiden standing over him, wielding a wooden bat aimed at his face. Wesley raised his arm to lessen the blow. He quickly rolled away from Aiden, although his body ached. He managed to get to his feet, but Aiden's bat caught his stomach, knocking the wind out of him, and then slammed his back again.

Did this guy intend to kill him?

He struggled to catch his breath, barely dodging the next blow. Blessed sirens sounded in the distance. Aiden threw the bat toward the bushes, then took off running.

Wesley groaned, then collapsed on the ground.

Shannon pressed her face to the window, but couldn't see anything from her vantage point. Where had Wesley and Aiden gone? She cupped her hand to her ear and tried to listen through the crack in the door. She heard nothing but sirens in the distance, so she slowly opened the door.

She glanced down and her face paled. *Oh no!*

"Wesley!" she shrieked.

TWENTY-SEVEN

Wesley grimaced as he attempted to turn over on his bed. Every inch of his body ached from head to toe. Had it been three days already since Aiden mistook him for a baseball? He couldn't imagine that being run over by a truck would feel much worse. Shannon's ex must *really* hate him. And if he admitted it to himself, he didn't exactly have warm fuzzy feelings for Aiden either. Especially after this.

"I know you wanted to teach me about charity, but you didn't have to demonstrate it by sacrificing your body."

He turned at Shannon's teasing words and tried to smile. He lifted his hand to take hers. "Anything for the love of my life."

"I still can't believe Aiden would do something like this." She frowned and lowered her head, which brought his attention to her work uniform.

"Going to work?"

"No, I just got off. I need to go pick up the kids at Christopher and Judy's. Your grandpa picked the boys up from the bus stop and took them home. But I had to stop by and see you."

"I'm glad you did, although I'm not that great of company right now."

"Oh, I don't know…" She leaned down, caressed his face, and rewarded him with a kiss. Her hand rested on his chest, radiating warmth through the thin sheet covering his torso. "I think I might like you at a disadvantage."

Her gentle touch almost made him forget about his pain. Almost.

"I hate being here. There's so much to do before Christmas. We didn't even put up your Christmas lights yet," he protested.

"That's okay. Christopher came over and put them up."

"My grandpa did? Really?"

"Your grandparents are so sweet. They have been so kind and helpful to the kids and me."

"I'm happy to hear that."

"You just need to get better."

"I'm sick of this bed."

She laughed. "You've only been there since yesterday."

"Plus a day in the hospital."

Her fingers glided over his arm. "I'm happy nothing was broken."

"Just a minor concussion and lots of bumps and bruises. And believe me, I'm feeling every one of them."

"I'm just glad Aiden's in jail." She chuckled. "His dad was so upset, he refused to bail him out."

"I guess he had to find out that he wasn't above the law. The hard way." He sat up and the sheet slipped from his torso. He caught Shannon staring and he kind of liked it, he admitted. He shouldn't, though. But there was no point in lifting it back up. "Help me up?"

He didn't actually need help. He just wanted her close.

"Are you…" She hesitated, as though not wanting to bring him pain. But the trouble was, *every* movement he made brought him pain. "Is it okay?"

He nodded. "It's fine."

She slipped her arm around his back to help him off the bed and he winced dramatically.

"Just kidding," he chuckled. "I'm in pain, but not *that* much."

She playfully nudged his arm and pursed her lips. "*You.*"

He grasped her wrist and pulled her close, dropping

his lips to hers. Before his cup of satisfaction could fill, a throat cleared from the doorway. He groaned and reluctantly broke away.

"Wesley!" Mom gasped as she stared at his bare chest.

He grunted as he pulled open a drawer and snagged a t-shirt. Very slowly and painfully, he finagled it over his head. He looked at his mom and grinned. "Happy now?"

"That's better. Now, out of the bedroom, you two. Scoot." She made a sweeping gesture with her hands.

"Yes, ma'am." Wesley sheepishly glanced at Shannon and mouthed, "Sorry."

Shannon giggled in response.

Shannon sat on the living room couch next to Wesley in his parents' home, with her handsome's fingers intertwined with hers. His parents sat opposite them, each in their own chair.

"Okay, you two. We need to have a talk." His mother headed up the conversation, but his father seemed to be in agreement.

"About?" Wesley's brow furrowed and he glanced at her.

"About doing things the right way." His father joined the conversation.

A puzzled expression flashed across Wesley's face, likely mirroring her own.

"The fact is, you two can't seem to keep away from each other," his mother said.

She was failing to see how that was a problem. Did they want them to spend less time together? To break up?

"And…?" Wesley frowned.

His father leaned forward. "And we think you need to get married. Sooner rather than later."

"What?" They both exclaimed at the same time.

"Mom, Dad…" Wesley's hand plowed through his hair. He grimaced as though the gesture brought him pain. "Listen, this is something Shannon and I need to decide on our own."

"I think the decision has already been made in both of your minds. Am I correct?" His father laced his hands together.

Wesley looked at her and they both nodded. "Yeah, but…"

"The Bible says it's better to marry than to burn. I've seen the way you look at her and the way she looks at you. You're burning. It's obvious to anyone with eyes," his dad stated.

This…was embarrassing. She must resemble a tomato.

"And with as much time as you two spend together, you will not be able to refrain. Trust us, we speak from experience." His mother nodded.

"But we've only known each other—"

"That doesn't matter. You're both good kids."

"Just wait." Wesley stood quickly and looked like he regretted it. "Let Shannon and me talk this over and decide for ourselves. I don't want her to feel pressured to marry me. Especially not like this. And contrary to popular opinion, I *can* demonstrate self-control."

"Like what I just saw in your bedroom?"

"We were kissing! Just kissing."

"Half dressed."

"*I* was half dressed. Shannon was fully clothed. And I had no intention of changing that. Probably couldn't even if I wanted to. At this point in time, I can barely move. I think she's pretty safe."

Shannon stood from the couch. "I should probably go. I told Christopher I'd pick up the kids before five."

"I'll walk you out." Wesley nodded.

They both hurried to the door and stepped outside.

Wesley closed the door behind them. "Shannon, I'm so sorry about that."

"A little funny and slightly embarrassing." She

laughed. "But I actually thought it was sweet."

"You did?"

"Is it really such a bad idea?"

"Wait. You…you would actually consider it?"

"I think I decided a week ago that I wanted to marry you. You're everything I could ever want in a man."

"Are…are you serious? Because if you are…" His hand worked through his hair again, accentuating his bicep. Not that she'd noticed. "I mean, I've already thought about it too. I just didn't think that you…"

She smiled. He was so adorable. "Well, I'm not particularly in a hurry. I can wait if I have to."

"But I want to do it the right way. At the right time. So, can we pretend like this whole episode with my parents never happened?"

"We can pretend, but I don't think I can ever forget. This is something we will want to tell our grandchildren about," she boldly said with a wink.

"Our grandchildren. I like the sound of that." He brought her close and kissed the top of her head.

TWENTY-EIGHT

Shannon had just tucked the children in bed. Now she sat alone in the living room, staring at the Christmas tree. Or more correctly, staring at the lack of contents under the tree. By this time, Mom would have had that whole bottom filled with colorful packages. Sorrow gripped her heart as tears began to fall.

She missed Mom and Dad so much. She wasn't sure how she was going to make it through this holiday season without them. How was she going to be able to hold it together in the presence of the kids? But maybe it was okay to cry. Maybe they needed to see the pain she was experiencing. Because, chances were, they were feeling the same emotions.

Wesley had written down a Bible verse and suggested that she read it whenever she was sad. She now held the Bible Wesley had given her in her lap and attempted to find the passage he had written down. She gave up her random searching, then flipped to the front to see if there was a table of contents. She found the correct book, turned to the page, then flipped to the chapter. Her eyes moved until they found the verse Wesley had written.

"He healeth the broken in heart, and bindeth up their wounds," she whispered the words aloud and soaked them into her soul.

"God, please heal our broken hearts."

Not even a minute after she uttered the prayer did a knock sound on the door. She quickly answered it before the kids awakened. Who could be visiting at this time of night?

"Wesley?" She looked behind him and saw Christopher and Judy as well. "What are you all doing here?"

Wesley shrugged. "They were getting out of their buggy when I pulled up. We didn't come together."

She smiled.

"I guess great minds think alike." Christopher chuckled.

"Come inside, before you turn into icicles." She urged them forward and moved out of the way.

Wesley carried a large cardboard box and set it down at his feet. He removed his coat and placed it on the hall tree.

She eyed his box.

"The gifts from the church. For the kids." He explained. "I'll put them under the tree, if that's okay."

"That's perfect." She wanted to melt in his arms.

Had God heard her pleas?

She turned to Christopher and Judy. "Would you like something to drink? Or a snack?" She gestured for the couple to take a seat.

"No, thank you," Judy said, leaning back on the couch.

"I could take some cookies and milk, if you can spare some." Christopher's grin stretched across his face.

Judy eyed his midsection. "You don't need any more cookies. Didn't you already get plenty today?"

"Just one then." Christopher winked at Shannon. "And a half glass of milk."

Judy seemed satisfied with his compromise.

Shannon returned to her guests in short order, with Christopher's treats in her hand. She handed a glass of milk and a couple of cookies to Wesley as well.

"Thank you." The way Wesley said the words caused her insides to tingle. As though he'd kissed her with just his words.

"*Denki*!" Christopher took a sip of his milk, spilling a little on his upper lip. It was then that Shannon noticed his lack of mustache. Had he shaved or did he always look that way?

"We can't stay too long. It's past Christopher's bedtime." Judy smiled, then looked at Christopher. "Do you want to tell her why we came, or should I?"

"We have something for you," Christopher said, handing her an envelope.

She stared at it. "What is it?"

"Open it." Christopher encouraged.

She did as told. Her eyes widened as she pulled out a stack of money. She didn't even count it, but the bill on just the top was one hundred dollars. "I can't take this." She shook her head.

"It is not our money. It is from the auction. Hundreds of people donated. It is for you and the *kinner*."

"The auction? But I—"

"Sometimes we have auctions to raise money for others in the community, if it's a special circumstance. We brought your situation before the leaders and we all agreed that this was something we wanted to do."

She shook her head. Was this really happening?

Wesley chuckled. "You're not going to be able to give that back. Just accept it."

"I can't believe you did this for us. Thank you so much. You don't know how much this means to me." She couldn't contain her tears of joy. Of relief. Of thankfulness. God truly cared.

She'd surely need to send a hearty "thank you" note to the Amish community.

"Look! I told you Santa was here! There's presents!" Jaycee came springing out of the hallway, with Brighton and Melanie close behind him.

"Presents!" Melanie squealed.

"It's not even Christmas yet, Jaycee," Brighton insisted.

"I know. But Santa's got lots of places to go. He just came here early. Huh, Santa?" Jaycee pointed to the coffee table. "See, he even has cookies and milk!"

Christopher simply looked at Judy and smiled.

"You three are supposed to be in bed. And you two have school tomorrow." Shannon reminded the boys.

"I can't wait to tell all my friends that Santa came early!"

Shannon shook her head. Then she and Wesley began laughing. Then Christopher and Judy joined in. Then each of the children.

Even little Melanie. She held up her ornament. "Baby Jesus on tree!"

Shannon smiled. "Are you ready to put your ornament on the tree?"

Melanie's little feet padded over to the tree and she set the ornament on a branch. "Baby Jesus on tree!"

Shannon's mind flashed back to a verse that she and Wesley had recently read together. It was about Jesus on a different tree—the one He'd died on as a man. Her gaze flew to Wesley and he smiled. Had he been thinking the same thing?

Christopher and Judy stood up. "Well, we don't want to prevent these little ones from getting the rest they need. We're going to head out now."

Shannon couldn't contain herself. She offered them both a hug of gratitude. Their appearance tonight made her think that maybe Jaycee's ideas weren't as outlandish as they seemed. She could see how he could equate this couple with Mr. and Mrs. Claus. But she knew better. It was the difference between fiction and reality.

No, it hadn't been Santa who had done all this. It was clearly God.

TWENTY-NINE

Christmas morning…

Ch'hristopher set his Bible down on the small table beside his hickory rocker. He eyed his *fraa* across the room. "I have been reading about the miracles of Jesus and noted something interesting."

Judy turned her attention to him. "What is interesting?"

"Sometimes *Der Herr* performs a miracle where you are. But sometimes He expects *us* to move, to do something about it, before He will send us a miracle."

"What do you mean?"

"The woman with the issue of blood in the Bible. She first had to touch the hem of His garment before she could be healed. The man born blind, he first had to call out to Jesus, then he was healed. See, *Der Herr* requires that first step of faith. And it is a step only we can take. And even if a situation is beyond hope, like that of Lazarus, He can still work a miracle."

She moved her glasses down her nose, then studied him. "What are you saying, husband?"

His hands shook, but his smile didn't falter. "I think we need to take that first step of faith."

Wesley excused himself after breakfast, bidding a temporary goodbye to his mom, dad, and his brother Randy who was visiting for Christmas break. Wesley had instructed his mother to keep an eye on the children until he and Shannon returned. Wesley pulled Shannon by the hand from the dining area.

"You were so right about the chocolate gravy and biscuits," she remarked.

"Aren't they the best?" He opened the door of his bedroom and ushered her inside, but kept the door ajar, for propriety's sake.

She sat on the edge of his bed.

"Here. I wanted you to open this with no one else around." He pulled a small gift-wrapped box out of his pocket.

She stared down at the small box. Was this…? No,

she wouldn't get her hopes up. It was still too soon.

"Go ahead. Open it," he urged.

She pulled off the wrapping paper and opened the small jewelry-size box. "Oh, Wesley!" She pulled out the pretty heart-shaped locket.

"It opens." He smiled.

She opened it up and stared down at a picture of her mother and father. Tears welled in her eyes. "Oh, Wesley. This is so special." She swiped at her tears. "Thank you. I love it."

He stared at her intently. "Do you love me?"

"Yes, of course."

"I love you too. More than just about anything or anyone." He reached for her hand and closed her fingers around something small, then dropped to his knee. "Shannon Parker, will you marry me?"

She squealed and threw her arms around him, nearly knocking him off balance. She kissed him on the lips, before they both rose to their feet. "Yes, Wesley Stoltz. I will most definitely and happily marry you!"

"Do you want to look at your ring now?"

Just when she thought her happiness meter couldn't go any higher, it did. She opened her hand to see the sweetest most dainty ring she'd ever seen. "It's adorable." She slipped it on her finger.

"I thought the style fit you perfectly, but if you were

hoping for a large rock, I can buy you one of those too."

"No, Wesley. This is absolutely perfect. It even fits my finger perfectly. How did you know?"

He shrugged. "I just guessed."

She heard Melanie's voice. "Should we go check on the kids now?"

"No, not yet. I need to kiss my new fiancée first." He pulled her close and claimed the kiss she'd been longing for all day.

A throat cleared loudly from the doorway.

Shannon and Wesley both began to giggle.

"Give us some slack, Mom. We're engaged now." Wesley grasped her hand, holding it up for his mother to see her ring.

"Engaged?" Apparently, he hadn't shared his plans with his mom.

His mom spun around and marched out of the room, then they heard her say, "Shannon and Wesley are now engaged! Woo hoo! We're gonna get grandbabies!"

Wesley chuckled. "I guess she's excited."

"I guess so." Shannon laughed.

He pulled her back into his arms again. "Now, where were we?"

Wesley glanced out the window when he saw the lights from a vehicle flash through the curtain. "Someone is here. Are we expecting more company?"

"Not that I know of," Mom said.

"I'll get the door," Wesley volunteered. He'd pretty much healed from most of the trauma Aiden wrought.

His mouth hung open the moment he answered the door. "Grandma? Grandpa?" In all his years growing up, not once had his grandparents visited. Not even on Christmas.

Dad stepped behind him. "*Daed*? Is everything okay?"

"*Ach*, everything is *chust* fine, *sohn*."

Wesley glanced at his father's puzzled expression.

"Why are you here?" Dad frowned.

"Won't you come in," Mom, who appeared the only one to be thinking clearly, offered.

"Yes, come in," Dad said, stepping around Wesley and opening the door wider.

Wesley moved away from the door and next to Shannon. He reached for her hand and gently squeezed it.

A fire kindled in his spirit. Something wonderful was happening at this moment, and he had a front row seat.

He shared a glance with his brother Randy, who

shrugged. Randy wasn't as close to their grandparents as Wesley was. Wesley had made an effort to get to know them, whereas Randy couldn't tolerate the "Amish drama" as he'd called it. But Wesley felt blessed to have a relationship with their grandparents.

It was only a matter of time before the children in the other room realized that "Santa" was there.

Grandpa and Grandma were led into the den, where they were offered their choice of seats. They chose the couch, likely because it was a luxury they weren't allowed to own.

Grandpa looked at Dad, his eyes misting. "*Mamm* and I have been talking. I have decided to go before the leaders and ask them to lift your *Bann*. I do not know what they will say, but I thought you would like to know."

Dad nodded graciously. "I will pray for a positive outcome and that God's will be done."

"We are praying that too," Grandma said as she accepted a mug of steaming coffee from Mom.

"Do they know you are here?" Dad asked.

"The *g'may*? *Nee*." Grandpa shared a loving look with Grandma, as though they were in on a special secret. "We are taking a step of faith."

"And hoping for a miracle," Grandma added.

The older adults chatted amongst themselves, while

Shannon and Wesley broke away. They peeked into the family room to check on the kids, who seemed entranced by their new gifts.

"Guess who's here," Wesley said with a grin. His gaze zeroed in on Jaycee.

Jaycee's eyes widened. "Santa!" He jumped up and ran out of the room, betraying the toys that had brought him enjoyment for the last half hour.

"Santa?" Melanie parroted.

"No, baby." Shannon smiled and took her hand. "It's Christopher and Judy."

Melanie clapped her hands. "Judy!"

"Come on, Brighton. I think Wesley's dad is going to read the Christmas story now." Shannon nodded toward the den.

They joined the rest of the family. Everyone took a seat and made themselves comfortable.

Wesley settled on the floor with his back against the sofa. His arm draped around Shannon's shoulders as she snuggled next to him.

Faces glowed with joy.

The fire crackled in the hearth.

The lights on the Christmas tree twinkled.

And Dad began reading the story of the first Christmas over two thousand years ago. The story of the birth of "Baby Jesus," who became the Saviour of the whole world. Who was literally born to die, demonstrating the ultimate act of charity. A costly love. Because God gave His very best, so that we might have the very best.

EPILOGUE

Six months later…

"Alright. Are your eyes still closed?" Wesley waved a hand in front of Shannon's face.

"Yes, they're closed. I'm going to fall asleep if I have to keep them closed any longer."

"We're almost there, I promise." Wesley cut the engine.

"May I open them?"

"Patience, wife." He leaned close and kissed her pretty face.

"I love it when you call me that. I don't think I'll ever get tired of it."

"Not even after four months of marriage?"

"Not even after four years of marriage. Or forty-four years."

He hopped out of the truck and jogged around the

247

front, then opened the door on the passenger's side. "I'm going to help you down. Keep your eyes closed until I tell you to open them."

He pulled her by the hand so she'd have a decent view. "Alright, open them!"

She did. Her mouth hung open. "Okay, Wesley. Tell me what I'm looking at."

"This, my dear wife, is our new home."

She screamed, half startling him in the process.

He laughed. "That was the reaction I was hoping for."

"You built us a cabin in the woods? This is exactly what I pictured. Exactly." She shook her head in apparent amazement.

"Do you like it?"

"It's gorgeous."

"There's a pond in back where the kids can ice skate when it gets really cold. I put up a fence around it, though, so it's not a danger to Melanie and whatever babies might come along."

Shannon's smiled widened. "Speaking of babies…"

"What? No! You're joking with me, right?"

She shook her head, then caressed his cheek. "Not joking. Daddy."

"Woo hoo!" He whisked her into his arms and carried her up the porch steps. "Oh, man. This might just be one of the happiest days of my life."

Sitting on their back porch, Shannon enjoyed watching the kids play in the yard. She glanced at her beloved. "I still can't believe all that's happened in such a short time. It's like I have a totally different life than I had last year at this time."

Wesley sipped his iced tea. "I hope you're happy."

"I am. You and your grandparents were such a Godsend. Really."

"Speaking of my grandparents, guess what."

"Was the *Bann* lifted?"

"Unfortunately, no." He frowned. "But my dad said that Grandma and Grandpa have been visiting them regularly."

"That's wonderful."

"What's even more wonderful is that they accepted Christ last week."

"Really? That's the best news ever!"

"It is." He smiled.

"I'm so glad I found Jesus. And you. And your grandparents. I truly don't know what I would have done without you guys in my life. I was so lost."

He reached for her hand. "I don't believe in coincidences. God put each of us in the right place, at the right time. Do you believe that?"

"I'm beginning to. It's strange to think that none of this would have happened if Mom and Dad hadn't died. It's almost like I had to let go of something precious to me to find something equally precious. And now, I couldn't imagine my life without having experienced both." She looked out at the children and smiled. "And to think, all this started because a little boy mistook an Amish man for Santa Claus. Who would have guessed?"

"God did. Well, He didn't guess. He knew it all along."

THE END

Thanks for reading!

To find out more about Jennifer Spredemann, join my email list, or purchase other books, please visit me at www.jenniferspredemann.com. My books are available in Paperback, eBook, and Audiobook formats. You may also follow Author Jennifer Spredemann on Facebook, Pinterest, Twitter, BookBub, Amazon, Instagram, and Goodreads.

Questions and comments are always welcome. Feel free to email the author at jebspredemann@gmail.com.

Dear Reader,

I sincerely hope *Unlikely Santa* touched your heart. I hope it is one of your favorite books this year. I hope you've fallen in love with Jaycee, Shannon, Wesley, and, of course, 'Santa.' But most of all, I pray you've fallen in love with JESUS, the true Reason for the Christmas season!

Blessings,

Jennifer Spredemann
Heart-Touching Amish Fiction

P.S. Word of mouth is the best advertisement. If you enjoyed this book, please tell a friend.

A SPECIAL THANK YOU

I'd like to take this time to thank everyone that had any involvement in this book and its production, including my Mom and Dad, who have always been supportive of my writing, my longsuffering Family—especially my handsome, encouraging Hubby, my Amish and former-Amish friends who have helped immensely in my understanding of the Amish ways, my supportive Pastor and Church family, my Proofreaders, my Editor, my CIA Facebook author friends who have been a tremendous help, my wonderful Readers who buy, read, offer great input, and leave encouraging reviews and emails, my awesome Launch Team who, I'm confident, will 'Sprede the Word' about *Unlikely Santa*! And last, but certainly not least, I'd like to thank my ***Precious LORD and SAVIOUR JESUS CHRIST***, for without Him, none of this would have been possible!

A special thank you to Janet D'Ambrise Steiniger, one of my readers who suggested the name Holly for Wesley's church friend. If you haven't joined my Facebook reader group, you may do so here: https://www.facebook.com/groups/379193966104149/

Thanks to my good friend and author, Tracy Fredrychowski, for her sugar cookie recipe. If you enjoy Amish fiction and haven't read her books, I suggest you pick up a copy of *The Secrets of Willow Springs*. Find more recipes like this one here:

https://tracyfredrychowski.com/sweettreat/

Stella's Drop Sugar Cookie Makes 4 dozen cookies

Ingredients:

1 cup powdered sugar

2 eggs

1 cup sugar

5 cups unbleached all-purpose flour

1 cup unsalted softened butter

1 tsp. salt

1 cup Canola oil

1 tsp. baking soda

2 tsp. pure vanilla

1 tsp. cream of tartar

Instructions:

1. Preheat oven to 350°
2. In large mixing bowl cream sugars, butter, oil, and vanilla until light and fluffy.
3. Add eggs one at a time and blend evenly.

4. In a separate bowl, sift together flour, salt, baking soda and cream of tartar.
5. Gradually add flour mixture to creamed mixture until blended.
6. Drop rounded 2" balls on ungreased cookie sheet. Flatten with bottom of a glass dipped in sugar.
7. Bake for 10-12 minutes, until edges turn golden brown. Allow cookies to cool on cookie sheet for 2 minutes before transferring to wire rack.

Discussion Questions for Unlikely Santa

1. At the onset of the story, Shannon is dealt an unfathomable tragedy, but manages to wade through it. Have you experienced a difficult situation in your own life? If so, how did you cope?

2. Shannon has difficulty providing for her family financially. Has there been a time in your life when you'd had to count your pennies, so to speak?

3. When Christopher encounters Jaycee, the boy misidentifies him. If you were in Christopher's shoes, would you have corrected Jaycee?

4. What was your first impression of Wesley? Aiden?

5. Have you ever purchased a meal for a stranger?

6. Shannon doesn't like depending on the charity of others. How do you feel about it? Have you ever

been in a situation that necessitated depending on the kindness of strangers?

7. When I first began writing this story, I had in mind for it to go a certain way. But, like most of my books, the characters have ideas of their own and highjack the story as Wesley and Aiden did. 😊 Did you suspect the story to play out the way it did? If not, how did you think the story would go?

8. This story was loosely based on a real-life incident of an Amish friend who was indeed mistaken for Santa Claus. Did you suspect the premise to be true?

9. Have you ever cut down a fresh Christmas tree?

10. Have you been to a place that celebrates Christmas like the Creation Museum? Have you ever been to a live nativity?

11. Did you grow up believing in Santa Claus? How did you react when you found out the truth?

12. Shannon eventually meets Jesus Christ, the true Reason for the Christmas season. Have you met Jesus? If so, do you remember when?

13. If you enjoyed this story, will you kindly consider leaving a review? Thanks!

Releasing February 1, 2020

The Trespasser

(Amish Country Brides)
©Jennifer Spredemann

Single mother Kayla Johnson embarks on a journey to Pennsylvania in search of her daughter's biological family. But when a storm forces them to turn in to an abandoned home in a small Indiana Amish community, Kayla must come to terms with her past disappointments and her distrust in God.

Amish widower Silas Miller has always dreamed of owning his own property. So when Minister Yoder vacates his home and moves out of state, Silas is thrilled to be caretaker for the Yoder homestead. When a trespasser finds shelter in the Yoders' house, Silas allows her to stay temporarily. Then Silas learns a secret that will not only rock his world, but challenge life as he knows it.

Will he listen to God's still small voice even if he's asked to give up his dream? An Amish romance to warm your heart and touch your soul.

Preorder Now!

A sneak peek at *The Trespasser*, coming 2020…

The Trespasser

Amish Country Brides

©2019-2020 Jennifer Spredemann

CHAPTER ONE

Kayla Johnson squinted to see through the windshield as her wipers attempted to keep up with the torrential downpour assaulting her vehicle. But even with the wipers at full speed, that proved to be a challenge. She wasn't even sure where she and Bailey were exactly, but they'd crossed the state line from Kentucky into Indiana about an hour ago, or so it seemed. She distinctly remembered the 'Welcome to Indiana' sign just as they'd crossed the bridge over the gigantic Ohio River.

Perhaps she should pull over somewhere and wait out the storm. She couldn't tell if she was even going the right way, since her GPS had lost its signal several miles back. She figured it was due to the storm raging outside. How long would this last? *Now* she understood when people mentioned the storms in the Midwest. This was downright terrifying.

As if on cue, a streak of lightning touched down just off to the left. Not even five seconds later, thunder shook her car. A shiver raced up her spine.

"I'm scared, Mommy," Bailey whimpered from her booster seat in the backseat.

Me too. "It's okay, baby. Mommy's going to pull off up here." She'd hoped to find a motel or a fast food restaurant, but who knew how far she was from one. The last town had several, but she'd spotted them before the sky began dumping buckets of water. She hadn't expected *this*. If she'd known this was coming, she would have reserved a hotel room in the last town, and she and her five-year-old daughter would be safe and sound, curled up under the covers watching a Hallmark movie.

She flipped on her signal and maneuvered onto the next street. Great, no lines to even mark the road? She must be out in the middle of nowhere. The vehicle crawled at a snail's pace as she struggled to see the road ahead of her. It seemed be at least a couple of inches deep in water. They really needed to get out of this. Was that a little store up ahead? She couldn't be sure since there were no lights on, but they were probably closed. 'Yoder's Country Market' the sign on the small white building read. *Amish?* As she pulled into the drive, she discovered a chain-link fence surrounding the parking lot. Definitely closed.

She sighed.

"I need to go to the bathroom," Bailey whined.

"Okay. I think there might be a house down this driveway. We'll stop and ask to use their restroom." She drove along what appeared to be a fenced pasture. Or was it a small pond? It was difficult to tell with all the water everywhere.

Her cell phone began vibrating. No doubt another storm warning. She briefly glanced at it. Flash flood warning. Great. Perhaps the residents would allow her and Bailey to stay a while. She hoped so, because being out in this weather set her nerves on edge.

She pulled up to a large white two-story house. Should she just stop in front, or find a place to park out of the rain? She opted for the latter when she noticed a couple of structures independent of the house. A barn and another outbuilding of some sort. She slowly crept up to the smaller structure, hoping there was an empty spot large enough to house her vehicle.

Thunder rumbled overhead once again.

"Please, Mommy! I gotta go!"

"Okay, baby." As soon as she pulled under the

outbuilding's roof, she could see clearly enough to park. She spotted a hitching post. *This must be where they park the buggies.* Except, there were no buggies present. Perhaps they were in the massive barn. Hopefully, the owners wouldn't mind her parking her car there.

Kayla opened the door, then went to release Bailey from her booster seat. "Do you think you can wait for Mommy to find the umbrella? It's just in my suitcase."

"I think so. But please hurry!" Bailey slid out of the car, then bounced up and down.

"I will." She quickly popped the trunk open and rifled through her clothing. She grabbed a comfortable change of clothes for each of them, just in case they were allowed to stay a while. "Okay. You ready to make a run for the door?"

"Yep."

"One. Two. Three." With the clothing tucked under her arm, she held the umbrella in one hand and Bailey's hand in the other, then made a mad dash for the front door.

"Whew!" She glanced down at her jeans near her ankles. They were completely soaked. It was a good thing she'd thought to grab extra outfits for the two of them. It would take a while for her tennis shoes to dry, however.

She knocked on the door loudly so it would be heard over the pounding rain. Didn't it ever let up? It seemed not.

No answer. She knocked again, harder this time.

"Mommy!" Bailey bounced.

"Okay, okay. I don't think anyone's home. I don't feel right just going inside."

"Maybe no one lives here anymore or they're on vacation like us." Bailey turned the knob, and the door opened. She rushed inside before Kayla could stop her.

"Bailey!"

"I have to go potty!"

Kayla gingerly stepped into the house and looked around. Indeed, it appeared empty. "Hello? Is anybody home?"

No answer.

"My daughter needs to use the restroom," she called out, stepping further inside. "Hello!"

Silence answered back. No one was home.

"Okay, we'll quickly find the bathroom, then we'll leave." She felt for a light switch but found none. *Oh, yeah. Amish. No electricity.*

A flash of lightning illuminated what appeared to be the living area, revealing sparse furniture covered in white sheets. It was as though the occupants had moved. But why would they leave the door unlocked?

"Where will we go?" Bailey's frightened voice commanded her attention once again.

"I don't know, baby. Maybe...let's just find the

bathroom so you don't pee your pants." She released a sigh of relief. If nobody was home, if the house was unoccupied, perhaps hunkering down here for an evening might be an option. But still, it wasn't her home. And how would she feel if a stranger occupied her place of residence in her absence? Not that she currently had a place of residence.

She walked through the darkened home. Thankfully, it wasn't pitch black. There should be a lantern somewhere, shouldn't there be? Perhaps not, if the owners no longer occupied the place. She scolded herself for not thinking to grab the flashlight out of the glove compartment. Of course, she hadn't expected to find an dark empty house. She'd run back out to get it if buckets of water weren't dumping from the sky.

She felt her way into the main living area until her eyes adjusted. Another flash of lightning revealed a kitchen off to one side. As she walked further inside the home, a quick perusal indicated a bedroom stood off to the other side, along a short hallway that led to stairs. Perhaps the bathroom adjoined the bedroom. She peered inside the empty room. No, it didn't appear to.

"I found it!" Bailey hollered.

A door slammed shut. Whew! At least now she didn't have to worry about Bailey having an accident.

Once her eyes adjusted a little more, she spotted a

lone lantern on a small table. Oh, good, a book of matches sat next to it. She quickly removed the hurricane glass, turned up the wick, then swiped a match to light it. A soft glow dispelled the darkness.

Fortunately, she'd come from a family of campers, so she was familiar with lighting lanterns, setting up tents, chopping wood, kindling a campfire, and other outdoor skills. Sadness filled her as she thought of Mom and Dad and all the wonderful times they'd spent camping. They'd passed away much too early. Did anyone survive cancer these days? It seemed not.

She briefly toured the lower level of the home with the lantern in hand, noting a few bedrooms. Two of them had lone beds in them, one covered by a quilt and the other with a plain comforter. Would the owners mind if she and Bailey occupied the rooms for a night? Since there seemed to be no one around to ask, she'd have to take a chance. What other choice did they have?

Thunder roared outside once again along with pounding rain. It appeared they wouldn't be going anywhere anytime soon. Not with all the flash flood warnings and lightning strikes. It just wasn't safe. Or smart.

Had Someone up above provided this shelter from the storm? It was possible, she supposed, but definitely not probable. The Man Upstairs didn't care about her or Bailey, she'd been certain of that since she first discovered her pregnancy. And then she'd lost both parents.

No, it certainly wasn't God. Finding this place had been pure luck, plain and simple.

CHAPTER TWO

S ilas Miller dashed for the shelter of the barn. He hated to take Strider out in this weather, but he needed to check the Yoders' gutters to make sure they were free of debris. It was times like this he was thankful his Amish community allowed enclosed buggies. The nearby Swiss Amish district, nicknamed the Swissies by local Plain folks, only utilized open-top carriages. He couldn't imagine weathering this menacing storm with a simple umbrella as protection. At least he was protected from the elements.

He quickly harnessed Strider, moved him between the traces, making sure to guide them into their proper places, and then pulled the leather reins into the buggy's cab. Fortunately, his horse loved the rain. Unfortunately, Strider did not love thunder and lightning.

Strider whinnied, excited to be leaving his barn stall, no doubt. He might have a change of mind once they got out onto the road and encountered a loud crash of thunder like the one several minutes ago. Maybe *Der Herr* would have mercy on poor Strider and hold off the lightning until they arrived at the Yoders'. He'd pray for that.

"Come on, boy. We won't be out too long, but it'll be enough to invigorate you." He gave the lines a gentle shake, urging Strider to begin their three-mile journey.

It seemed like the rain had let up a tiny bit, but it still poured. He just hoped the driver of the car up ahead spotted him and slowed down. This road was quite narrow and, in some places, had no room to pull off to the side. He double checked to make sure his blinking lights were on. He pulled to the right as much as possible to allow the car to pass.

He sighed in relief once it did. Hopefully, no one else was crazy enough to be out in this weather. He wouldn't be either, but he'd promised Dan Yoder that he'd look after his place after their family had moved back to Pennsylvania. Dan, the minister of their district, had talked about selling the place on more than one occasion, but for whatever reason, it had yet to go up for sale. And for that, Silas was happy. He'd dreamed about having his own acreage, complete with a large barn, and a small store in the front, since he'd been finished with school. The Yoders' property would be the perfect place, but he was in no position finance-wise to buy it. Nowhere near, actually. But he had been saving his money. And praying that the house wouldn't sell to anyone else.

As he neared the two-mile mark, he noticed something up ahead. *Ach,* the creek had swollen considerably.

"Do you think we can do it, Strider?"

The horse lifted his head as though in agreement.

"Okay, but we'll have to be careful."

He approached the water cautiously and urged Strider along. "Come on, boy. You can do this." He slapped the reins a little firmer. "Let's go!"

The horse waded through the water adequately, but the buggy weighed still him down. Silas encouraged the horse again and glanced out the side flap. The water reached the middle of his buggy's wheel. If it were any higher, Strider wouldn't be able to pull through.

Once they were safely past the creek, he exhaled in relief. It proved to be swifter than he'd surmised. Getting back home would be a chore if the creek rose any higher. As a matter of fact, maybe he'd use the Yoders' phone shanty and leave a message on the line closest to his folks' place. That way, if they worried about him, they'd check the answering machine before heading out into the foul weather in search of him.

Staying overnight at the Yoders' place would almost seem like a mini vacation. And he could dream of the future when he—*Gott* willing—owned the place. He smiled at the thought. *Jah*, that was what he'd do.

He stopped at the phone shanty at the end of the lane when he'd driven in, and left a message. Hopefully, *Mamm* wouldn't worry about him. Ten minutes later, he pulled into the drive. He led Strider to an empty stall in the barn, then filled a bucket with water and offered the horse some grain he kept stored in the corner.

He stood looking toward the house, waiting for a break in the rain. After a few minutes, he realized he might not get one. As a matter of fact, it was coming down even harder than when he'd pulled in. He was just glad he'd been able to arrive before the lightning struck. Now that Strider was securely in the barn, he'd settle in for the night. He'd have to wait until the rain died down a little bit to check the gutters.

He wished he'd thought to bring an umbrella. It certainly would have made his escape to the house a bit more pleasant. And dry.

Silas pushed the door open and immediately removed his boots. He paused for a moment, midstride as he walked through the living room. Had he heard something? It was difficult to determine above the rain pounding on the metal roof. He'd always loved the sound. How many nights had he fallen asleep to it?

He reached for the lantern on the table. Except it wasn't there. He could have sworn that he'd left it in the same place he always did—not that he'd ever really swear. As he allowed his eyes to adjust to the dim interior, he noticed something peculiar. Faint light seeped from the bedroom door, which seemed to be cracked open. The hairs on his arms raised. Was someone inside the house?

His heart began pounding. Who could be here? Dan Yoder hadn't said he was returning, so it must be an intruder. He quietly tiptoed toward the bedroom door, then put his ear to the crack. Sure enough, someone or something was in that bedroom.

All at once, he forced the door open and burst into the room. "What are you doing here?"

"Ah!" A woman, who stood in only her undergarments, quickly pulled the bed quilt around herself.

Jah, that had been a mistake. Too bad he'd realized it too late. His face burned. "I…I'm sorry…you just…uh, *jah*…I'll…I'll just go…out." He turned around as quickly as he'd entered. *Oh, man. What have I done?*

Silas paced the living room, trying to determine his next course of action. Had he *really* just burst in on a woman while she was changing? *Ach! Dummkopp.*

A few moments later, the woman—fully dressed now—walked into the room. "I'm sorry that you…" She shook her head. "This is a little awkward."

He nodded. *Jah*, it certainly was. He had no words.

"My daughter and I were out driving in the storm. She needed to use the facilities, so we stopped in here, thinking someone would be home. We'd only planned to use your restroom and then be on our way to search for a hotel, but they'd sent out flash flood warnings and my GPS lost its signal. And frankly, I don't even know where we are." She glanced toward one of the bedrooms. "My daughter is sleeping already. But we can leave if you'd like us to…uh, Mr. Yoder."

"Oh, I'm not Dan Yoder. My name is Silas Miller. I live down the road a spell. I'm tending Yoder's farm while he's gone."

Preorder your copy now!

Made in the USA
Monee, IL
21 May 2020